Moon Wreck

Raymond L. Weil

DEDICATION

To my wife Debra for all of her patience while I sat in front of my computer typing. It has always been my dream to become an author. I also want to thank my children for their support.

CONTENTS

Moon Wreck: First Contact: Page 1
Moon Wreck: Revelations: Page 33
Moon Wreck: Secrets of Ceres.   Page 78

Moon Wreck: First Contact

Chapter One

Mission Commander Jason Strong stared at the damaged lunar lander with a sick feeling in the pit of his stomach. His best friend and copilot Greg Johnson was standing next to him. They both wore cumbersome white spacesuits suited to the lunar environment. All Jason could hear was Greg's heavy breathing coming over the suit radio. He was also having a hard time keeping his own breathing steady. The landing had been a disaster. There were no backup plans for what had happened. They were stranded on the Moon with no way home.

"Damn!" Greg finally said in an unsteady voice. "We're really screwed now. How could this happen?"

Both men were staring at their lunar lander, which was lying on its side at the edge of a small crater. The crater was only four to six feet deep, but that had been enough for one of the lander's support struts to become unstable and the lander to topple over.

"I don't see any way to right it," commented Jason, thinking about what they needed to do and the equipment they had available to them. "Nobody ever considered this scenario."

"How about the mechanical arm on the rover?" asked Greg, sounding desperate. "Could we use it to set the lander back up?"

He had a wife and infant son back home. He didn't want her to have to raise their son by herself. He could just imagine how she was feeling. There had been no contact with Mission Control for over twelve hours. Down on Earth, they would know something had gone terribly wrong. He could imagine the people in Mission Control frantically trying to contact them and only getting silence back in return. They had lost all contact just a few minutes into their descent.

"Not strong enough," replied Jason, shaking his head. "The lander just weighs too much. Even in the lighter lunar gravity it's too much for the mechanical arm on the rover."

"Then we're going to die here," responded Greg glumly. He walked over to the lander in a shuffling gate and put his white gloved hand against the small American flag on the side of the lander. It had been his lifelong dream to travel to the Moon. "We're the first manned mission to the Moon in decades, and we crashed. It will be years before there is another."

Jason walked over to stand next to Greg. He reached out and put his hand on his friend's shoulder. The open hatch to the lander was just above them. They were fortunate the hatch had remained unblocked, or they would have been trapped inside. "Any chance of getting the radio working?"

"The antennas are crushed," replied Greg, pointing toward the front of the lander, which was leaning against a large dark boulder. The boulder had put a sizable dent in the side of the lander. They were fortunate it hadn't penetrated the hull. "Not only that, but that mysterious interference we detected on our descent will screw up any radio signal we try to transmit."

"That damn interference shut down our computers," spoke Jason, recalling the harrowing descent when most of the lander's systems had suddenly shut down.

It had been all he could do to stabilize the lander and finish the descent to the surface. Without the advanced LIDAR ranging system on line and computers, they had to resort to old fashion radar. Unfortunately, the radar system was intermittent due to the powerful interference coming from the Moon. Greg had to look out the lander's viewports to guide Jason down the last several hundred feet. Because they couldn't see or detect what was directly below them, they had crashed in the small crater.

Jason was silent for a moment as he weighed their options. None were good. "We have enough air in the lander to last several weeks; if we can get power to the recycler our oxygen supply will last for several months."

"The batteries are fully charged, and the emergency fuel cells are intact," responded Greg, sounding slightly calmer. He had checked those before they had exited the lander. "But that still leaves the question of what we do about food and water. Even on emergency rations, we only have enough for about three weeks."

"Can we get the rover out?' asked Jason, walking over to stare at the bottom of the lander and the compartment that held the lunar rover. He had a plan that he had been considering. Somehow, he had to find a way to get them off the Moon and back to Earth.

"I don't see why not," replied Greg, coming to stand next to Jason and staring up at the rover's shielded compartment. "It's light enough in the Moon's gravity that we should be able to position it properly if there's a problem. I don't see any obvious damage to the rover compartment. Why do you want to get the rover out? It's sort of pointless. I mean, why do any exploration? We can't get back to Earth!"

Jason turned to face Greg. He knew Greg was worried about his wife and son. "Something is causing the interference that screwed up our landing. It's still preventing any radio signals from getting out. Don't forget that the rover has a radio that is capable of reaching our orbiting command module. We just need to find what is causing that interference and shut it down."

"You think it's artificial?" Greg asked in surprise, his eyes growing wide. This was something he hadn't considered. "How can that be possible? We would have known if there had been another mission heading for the Moon. You can't keep something like that a secret."

"The interference has to be artificial," responded Jason, looking off toward the south. "It didn't start until we began our descent. To me that's too big a coincidence. I don't think it was a manned mission. As you said, something like that couldn't be kept a secret."

"You think another country snuck a probe up here hoping to screw up our landing so our company couldn't get the space contract?" Greg asked with doubt in his voice. He just didn't see how it could have been done in secret.

He knew that a smaller rocket would have been harder to detect, but it still would have been difficult to land a probe on the Moon without it being noticed. Not only that, but they had kept their landing site a secret until the day of the launch.

"What else?" Jason replied with growing conviction in his voice. "This exploration contract for the Moon and Mars is worth potentially hundreds of billions of dollars. There are even companies in our own country that would like to see us fail."

"It would have cost a hell of a lot of money to get a probe to the Moon just to sabotage us," Greg replied doubtfully. "But I can see how the space contract would have made it tempting. With our failure, there are several other companies that will be jumping in to get their share." Greg was silent for a moment as he mulled everything over.

"So, do we get the rover out and go looking for the source of the interference?" Jason asked once more. While Jason wasn't married, he still had a brother and sister he would like to get back to Earth to see. He also knew that Greg wanted desperately to get back to his family.

"I guess it's better than sitting around here waiting for our air to give out," Greg replied after thinking about it for several moments.

"If we can shut down the interference, we can contact Mission Control from the rover. If they know where we are, there's a good possibility our company can send a supply drone to the Moon. It would allow us to replenish our supplies and survive until our people down on Earth figure something out."

"They could even send us something to set the lander back up," Greg spoke with some excitement flowing into his voice. "If we can right the lander, we can go home!"

"Perhaps," replied Jason, looking up into the star-studded sky. The Earth was plainly visible above the distant lunar horizon. "Let's not get ahead of ourselves. We still have a lot to do and even if we can contact Earth, we may be on the Moon for quite some time."

The two climbed back up into the lunar lander and shut the hatch behind them. After a few moments, they had the small airlock pressurized, and they opened the inner hatch to the inside compartment. Helping each other out of their cumbersome spacesuits and stowing them away, the two crawled over to their acceleration couches and sat down. Due to the way the lander had fallen over they were in a reclining position, but all the controls were still within easy reach.

"Anything on communications?" Jason asked, still hoping that the interference would come to a stop on its own. They still had short-range communications from an internal antenna.

Greg pressed several buttons and flipped multiple switches, but all that came over the speakers was static. The same thing they had heard for the last twelve hours.

"No, same as before," Greg replied disappointed. "It looks as if we're going to have to take that trip to wherever this interference is coming from."

Jason was silent for a moment. He could see the worry on Greg's face. He knew that his best friend was thinking of his family back down on Earth.

"Don't worry Greg, we'll get out of this," Jason said determinedly. "Once we find the probe that is broadcasting this interference and shut it down, we can arrange a rescue. We will also make sure whoever sent that probe is taken care of. I will personally make sure their company is put out of business."

"Let's just find that probe first," replied Greg, reaching forward and dimming the lights in the cabin. He lay back on his acceleration couch and looked over at Jason. "I still find it hard to believe that someone would intentionally sabotage our landing."

"Mission Control should be picking up this interference," Jason commented as he mentally went over the companies, and even countries, that might have sent the probe.

"Possibly," Greg spoke in agreement. "But there is nothing they can do. The source of the problem is here on the Moon, not down on Earth."

"We'll break the rover out in the morning," responded Jason, knowing they both needed some sleep. "It shouldn't take us too long to find the source of the signal."

"I hope so," replied Greg, reaching into his pocket and taking out a photograph of his wife and baby. He looked at his family in the dim light. He swore to himself he would do whatever was necessary to make it back home to them.

Jason tried to relax, knowing they would have a strenuous day coming if they succeeded in getting the rover out. Jason had been a military test pilot for six years before retiring and applying for the job of chief pilot for the new space company that Greg and he now worked for. His sister had been against him volunteering for this mission. She had said it was too dangerous, especially with a new space vehicle built by a private company. She had reminded him that if something happened on the Moon, there would be no one to rescue them.

His brother had been excited and slapped Jason happily across the back when he found out that Jason had been chosen as chief pilot and mission commander. His sister had been very quiet and had gone into another room for a while. She eventually came back out and wished him good luck, knowing this was what Jason had always wanted. However, Jason could tell from his sister's demeanor that she really didn't want him going to the Moon.

Jason closed his eyes and tried to sleep. His sister had been right, and now Greg and he were stranded on the Moon with no way home. Jason knew that his sister would be at Mission Control and would not leave until she heard something. Her husband was currently overseas working as a consultant for an oil company. He wasn't due back for another month. Someway, Jason had to find a way home. He couldn't let his sister down.

Jason and Greg had gotten up early and were out working diligently on the hatch to the rover compartment. It hadn't been designed to be opened from a nearly horizontal position. After a little work, they managed to get the hatch open and secured so they could get to the rover.

The rover slipped out of its compartment a lot easier than Jason had expected. A little pushing and shoving and they had it positioned far enough away from the obstructing landing struts that it could be activated.

Jason stepped forward and pressed a large recessed button on the side of the rover. Instantly the rover unfolded, and the six large wheels rotated around until they were touching the lunar surface. It looked just like a giant spider unfolding its legs.

"That was easier than I expected," commented Greg, looking at the rover.

"I don't see any damage," Jason replied. The rover compartment was well shielded, and the crash didn't look as if it had harmed it.

Jason walked slowly around the rover, carefully inspecting it. The rover was a fully contained vehicle with a nuclear power source furnished by the American government. It was equipped with cameras and communication equipment that would allow them to communicate with either the lander or the orbiting command module.

Stepping over to the controls on the small instrument panel, Jason checked the dials. Power was operational, oxygen supplies were topped out, and the onboard guidance computer was flashing a warning light. Just like the computers in the lander, the one on the rover was experiencing problems with the mysterious transmission.

"Same as the lander," muttered Greg, noticing the blinking light. "I guess it was to be expected."

"Yeah; same as the lander," replied Jason, looking over at Greg. "But everything else checks out."

"So what do we do now?" Greg asked, perplexed. "How do we navigate without the guidance computer?"

The computer had a three dimensional map of the lunar surface programmed into its memory. Normally all they would have to do was plug in their destination and the rover would drive them to it.

"I guess we do it the old fashioned way," Jason replied. It didn't seem as if they could catch a break. "We have detailed maps, which show the lunar surface. We can use them."

Greg looked toward the south. Navigating would not be easy. There were several craters and small hills between them and the source of the interference. Without the navigational computer, the trip was bound to take longer.

Greg hated leaving the safety of the lander. At least inside of it, they had some comforts. Food, water, air, power, and they could take off their spacesuits. The lunar rover had two seats and hookups so they could run their spacesuits off the rover's power system. There was also a small air recycling system that could regenerate their air.

"Let's go inside, get a little rest, eat, and then we can head toward the source of the transmission," Jason suggested. He knew they needed to be doing something to take their minds off their precarious situation.

"That source is approximately thirty miles away," Greg responded still looking toward the south. "Even with the rover, that's going to be a long trip." He kicked his foot at the lunar surface and watched the lunar dust fly up. "There's an awful lot of this damn dust everywhere. I hope it doesn't screw up the rover."

"All the moving parts are shielded against the dust," Jason reminded Greg as he walked back over to the side of the lander where the open hatch was waiting.

"Are we doing the right thing?" asked Greg, stopping just below the hatch and looking at Jason. "There's still a chance the lander could be spotted by Earth based telescopes. They could already be in the process of sending a supply drone."

Jason paused. This was something he had already considered. "Possibly," he admitted. "But why put all of our eggs in one basket? If we can find the source of the interference and shut it down, we can easily contact Earth. The telescopes on Earth might have a hard time spotting the lander. After all, it's lying on its side at the edge of this small crater. That will make it more difficult to see. We're also over fifty miles away from our planned landing site. Even if they can spot us from Earth, it may be days before they do so."

"You're right," Greg admitted with a heavy sigh. "Our best bet is to find the source of the interference. Let's get back inside the lander."

With a little help, Jason climbed into the open hatch and then leaned out to pull Greg up. Soon the two were back inside the lander.

After getting their spacesuits off, Jason settled down in his acceleration couch and pulled down a detailed map of the Moon. He had spent several hours earlier pouring over the map, calculating the most likely position for the source of the interference. A red x was marked in a crater approximately thirty miles away in a southerly direction.

Jason turned to Greg. "You don't have to go," he reminded him. "I can handle this by myself."

"Yeah; stay here in this lander alone and I will go space happy," spoke Greg, shaking his head. "I would rather take my chances with you. Besides what would your sister say if something happened to you and I was safe back here in the lander? How would I ever explain that to her?"

Jason smiled at Greg. His sister definitely wouldn't be happy about that. If they made it back to Earth, Jason knew he would get a long, I told you so, lecture from his sister. If they made it back, that lecture would be worth it.

The two settled down, ate a light meal, and drank some of their precious water. They lay quietly on their couches, both lost in their own private thoughts.

Greg finally stood back up and made his way over to his spacesuit. "No point in delaying this."

"You're right," responded Jason, moving over to help Greg put on his cumbersome spacesuit. Once Greg's suit was on, Greg helped Jason with his.

A few minutes later, they were both back out on the lunar surface. Jason took his seat in the vehicle and Greg climbed in beside him. They had both spent many long hours training in the rover in the Arizona desert. Their training was now about to be put to the test.

"Let's go," said Greg, buckling the harness that secured him inside the rover.

Jason pressed the accelerator, and the rover began to move. Jason drove slowly at first, trying to get the feel of driving in the light lunar gravity. He had to be careful to avoid small boulders and the occasional shallow crater. After a few minutes, Jason began to feel more at ease driving the rover over the desolate lunar surface.

"Just like driving a car," quipped Jason, trying to sound lighthearted. He knew that Greg was still extremely concerned about his family.

"Without shocks," groaned Greg as they hit a small rock.

For several hours, Jason drove the rover across the rough lunar surface. He carefully picked his way between the boulders and small hills that blocked their path. After each detour, he always came back to a bearing of due south.

"What do you think we will find?" asked Greg, breaking the silence. "Do you think the probe was sent from a country, or a rival company?"

"I don't know," Jason responded as he drove around a small boulder, stirring up more lunar dust. "It just doesn't make a lot of sense if you really think about it."

"What do you mean?" asked Greg, looking over at Jason feeling puzzled.

Jason hesitated as he tried to organize what he wanted to say without worrying Greg too much. "I can't see the probe being from another country. It could cause some serious international problems if it was ever discovered that our landing had been sabotaged. I'm not sure any of the ones wanting to reach the Moon and Mars would risk that."

"What about another company?" asked Greg, agreeing with Jason's assessment of other countries probably not being involved. "Do you have any in mind that might want to take us out in order to get one of the contracts?"

"A couple, possibly," responded Jason, thinking about the half dozen rival companies that were competing for shares of the lucrative space contracts. "There are only two that might be willing to take such a risk. What surprises me is that no one detected the probe being launched."

"It could have been launched from a ship out on the ocean," suggested Greg, trying to think of how a launch could have been accomplished in secrecy.

"Possibly," Jason said. "Even then, it should have been detected. Someone should have noticed. There are a number of tracking stations that should have picked up an ocean launch."

"Or they didn't mention it," added Greg, knowing that money sometimes had an extremely long reach. "Someone could have been paid to look in the other direction."

"It's a possibility," Jason replied as he drove the rover up the slope of a small hill and then back down the other side. So far, the rover was responding very well.

-

Three hours later, Jason brought the rover to a stop at the base of a long ridge. He looked to his left and then to his right, seeing that the ridge extended as far as his eyes could see.

"I don't think the rover can climb over that," commented Greg, frowning. "It's too steep."

"Way too steep," Jason replied in agreement. Everything had been going too smooth. He should have expected to run into some type of obstacle.

He took out the map of the lunar surface for this area of the Moon. It was difficult to unfold with his thick, insulated gloves. After struggling for a moment, he finally succeeded in opening the map. He gazed at what he thought was their location. The suspected location of the interference was in a crater just on the other side of the obstructing ridge. He had noticed the ridge while still in the lunar lander, but he had hoped to find a way to cross it with the rover.

"Looks as if we're walking," muttered Greg, reaching forward and unbuckling his safety harness. They had come too far to turn back now. "It's time to find out what's causing this interference."

"Make sure your oxygen tank and power supply are topped off," spoke Jason, agreeing with Greg's assessment. They would have to walk from here. If the map was correct and he had properly pinpointed the location of the interference, they had about a mile to go.

Jason reached forward and unbuckled his safety harness. As he did so, he checked his oxygen supplies and suit power levels. Both were topped out and should last for six hours, there was also a two-hour emergency supply if needed.

The two men exited the rover and walked over to the base of the ridge. It wasn't too terribly steep. However, the rover wasn't designed to climb such a slope. Being careful, the two began their ascent. They had to watch for loose rocks and small patches of lunar dust. Some of the dust was several inches thick in places. More than once, they dislodged small stones and caused patches of dust to begin sliding down the ridge. Due to the low gravity on the Moon, everything moved as if it were in slow motion.

Jason was the first to reach the top of the ridge. He turned and grabbed Greg's hand, pulling him up the last several feet. Then they both turned and looked down at the crater in front of them trying to spot the probe. From the top of the ridge, Jason knew it should be easily visible.

"Oh my God!" Greg spoke, his eyes growing very wide. He felt a cold chill run down his back. "It can't be!"

Jason looked down at the crater and the massive amount of wreckage strung across it. This was a crash site. A crash site that extended for nearly a mile, with mangled wreckage everywhere. It ended at the far side of the crater. Jason felt stunned by what was in the crater.

On the far side of the crater were the remains of an extremely large spacecraft. Only the front section of the spacecraft seemed to be intact. The rest was scattered across the crater. Jason estimated that the intact front section must be nearly four hundred feet long and two hundred feet wide.

"That wasn't built on Earth," Greg spoke quietly. He could feel his heart pounding in his chest. This was the last thing he had expected to find. Hell, he hadn't even considered this possibility.

"No, it wasn't," agreed Jason, wondering what to do next. It had taken them nearly forty minutes to climb to the top of the ridge. He figured it would take another twenty minutes to climb down and about thirty more to reach the main part of the wreckage.

"I wonder how long it's been here?" asked Greg, trying to estimate how big the spacecraft had been from all the wreckage scattered in the crater.

"For quite some time," responded Jason, turning to look at Greg. "A crash like this and all the dust it would have stirred up would have been spotted from Earth. For all we know, this thing has been here for hundreds of years or even longer."

"What do we do now?" Greg asked, still gazing at the wreck. Exploring a crashed alien spaceship wasn't in his job description. But did they have any other option? "That ship must still have an active power source and some type of working transmitter on board that's causing all the interference."

"We have no choice," answered Jason, trying to sound calmer than he felt. "We go down there and see if anyone's home."

"You think someone might have survived that crash?" Greg asked, taken aback at the thought. Greg didn't know if he was prepared for a first contact scenario. "You think someone in that wreck activated the transmission that caused us to crash?"

"I doubt it," replied Jason, looking at the wreckage. "This was a very bad crash. I don't think anyone could have survived. That transmission didn't start until after we began our descent. It might be some type of emergency beacon that was activated when our lander came within range."

"An emergency beacon!" Greg said, worriedly his eyes looking upward toward the stars. "I wonder who they are signaling."

"Probably no one," said Jason, trying to sound confident. "That wreck's been here for too long. If someone had been searching for it, they are long gone."

"I hope so," responded Greg, gazing back down into the crater. Here they were stranded on the Moon with a wrecked alien spacecraft. Could the situation get any worse?

"Let's go," said Jason, starting down the steep slope. "The sooner we get there, the better."

Greg followed Jason down the crater wall. Every so often, he glanced at the alien shipwreck. He felt an icy chill run up and down his back at the thought of what they might find. They had just learned a startling fact, one most astronomers had always predicted: they were not alone in the universe.

Chapter Two

Jason and Greg quickly descended the steep slope, being careful not to trip or stumble. They had to work themselves carefully around boulders and avoid the steeper areas. Their protective, bulky spacesuits made this difficult, and they had to be careful not to trip and fall. Neither of them wanted to roll uncontrollably down the slope and risk tearing or damaging their spacesuits. They finally reached the bottom of the ridge and headed off for the first large piece of wreckage. It was about one hundred yards from the base of the ridge.

"It looks like the ship came in low over the ridge and then hit here," stated Jason, glancing at a shallow depression in the ground. "It was a rough landing."

The depression hadn't been that noticeable from the top of the ridge. From the crater floor, it was obvious the spacecraft had struck the crater floor with some force and then slid all the way across, coming to a stop nearly a mile away at the far wall of the crater. The force of the impact had caused tremendous damage to the ship.

"This definitely happened a long time ago," commented Greg, gazing at the wreckage and the indentation in the ground. He had an advanced degree in geology and several other sciences. "When the ship struck, it must have sent a cloud of dust high above the lunar surface. When the dust fell back down, it covered everything with a thin, camouflaging layer. That's why this wreck isn't visible from Earth."

They reached the first big piece of wreckage and stopped to examine it. It was about twenty feet across and looked to be part of the ship's hull.

Jason reached out and put his gloved hand against the strange looking surface. It was slightly pitted; another indication it had been here for quite some time. The pitting had probably been done by micro meteors. The piece of metal itself had a slight curve to it and several large dents, probably caused by hitting the lunar surface.

"This metal's about twelve to fourteen inches thick," commented Greg, looking at one of the rough edges. "That seems awfully thick for a spacecraft. Why would they use such thick hulls? It would make the weight of the entire ship nearly astronomical."

"It's a big ship," replied Jason, looking around at all the scattered wreckage.

From the looks of the wreckage around them, a large part of it seemed to be from the ship's hull. There was a much larger piece several hundred feet away that seemed to have some sort of rocket engine attached.

Jason and Greg walked over to the larger piece and stood, mystified. It resembled a rocket engine, but it was unlike any they had ever seen before. It obviously didn't burn any type of chemical fuel.

Greg examined the rocket engine section for several minutes before turning to face Jason. "Whatever this thing used for power, it's far greater than anything we have ever thought about. I would guess we are looking at nuclear fusion, or perhaps even anti-matter."

"I'm not surprised," responded Jason, wondering what type of advanced science they were dealing with. He was familiar with numerous theories about advanced spacecraft design and what would be needed for power. This looked as if it was far beyond anything that he had studied. "Look how large this ship is. Conventional power sources like those that we use currently would never be able to move it. It has to be something exotic."

"There's a lot to learn here," Greg spoke in sudden realization. "We could advance several fields of science by hundreds of years from what is in this crater." He turned and faced the larger, nearly intact front portion of the ship. "Jason, do you realize that there is no way this ship ever originated in our Solar System? The secret to interstellar travel may be waiting for us over in that front section of the ship." Greg had always dreamed of someday traveling to the stars. He felt a thrill of excitement run up his back as he realized that tantalizing secret might be resting right here in front of him.

"Don't get your hopes up too high, Greg," Jason cautioned. He knew why Greg was feeling so excited. He was feeling the same way. "We don't know what the inside of the ship may be like. Keep in mind that we are on the Moon, not down on Earth. This ship will be very difficult to study. We also need to find the transmitter that is sending out that signal or the people down on Earth will never know what's here."

"You're right," Greg replied with a heavy sigh. "But the transmitter is working, and that means there is still some power in that wreck. That front section looks mostly intact."

"I wonder why they crashed?" asked Jason, looking at Greg. "A ship as advanced as this one evidently was should not have crashed on our moon."

"The more complicated a ship becomes the more likely it is for problems to pop up," Greg replied. "It could have been a navigational error or some type of serious mechanical problem with the ship. We may never know why they crashed."

"Let's go on to the main section," suggested Jason, gesturing toward the crater wall where the front of the wrecked spacecraft was. "We're not going to find any answers out here."

The two began walking across the crater toward the main part of the wreckage. They had to be careful because there were numerous pieces of wreckage laying everywhere and some of those were quite jagged. It would be easy to fall and rip a hole in one of their spacesuits. After carefully making their way through the field of wreckage, they found themselves at the main part of the wreck.

"My God, it's huge!" Greg spoke in awe, staring upward. The wreck towered above him. "It's over one hundred feet high."

"It must have had a large crew," added Jason, trying to imagine the technology it would take to build such a large spaceship. "I wonder where this ship came from and how it ended up here on the Moon? The bodies of its crew could still be inside."

"Bodies?" uttered Greg, stepping back away from the wreck. That was something he hadn't considered. He looked at Jason with sudden worry. "What do you mean, bodies?"

"If no rescue ship ever came, there will be bodies inside," replied Jason, looking at Greg. He was surprised that Greg hadn't realized this possibility.

The thought of finding alien bodies made Greg feel uneasy. Was it right for them to enter what was in reality an alien tomb? However, what other choice did they have? The transmitter inside had to be shut down. Greg took a fortifying breath. He knew they had to go inside.

Greg looked along the hull of the ship. There were several hatches visible above them on the higher levels, but none down where they were. "I don't see any way in."

"Let's walk around this section of the wreck," Jason suggested. "There has to be an entry somewhere. We just need to find it."

One thing Jason had noticed immediately was the conspicuous absence of portholes. The hull was solid except for what looked like numerous indentations and hatches. Why were there so many hatches?

The two slowly walked around the massive wreck. It was obvious that several large explosions had occurred in the rear section, but there was so much tangled and loose metal that Jason didn't feel it was safe

15

to enter. On the far side, they finally came to a hatch that was within easy reach. It was about fifteen feet high and about the same width.

There was a large handle on the hatch at chest level, and Greg reached out and pulled on it. He nearly stumbled and fell as the hatch swung easily open. "It's not sealed!"

"No," responded Jason, looking inside. The inner hatch door was partially open. "This might be an indication that a rescue ship did come and the surviving crew was evacuated. That could be why we saw no bodies outside."

"That's great!" Greg said with obvious relief in his voice. "No live aliens and no bodies."

"I said it might indicate a rescue," Jason reminded him.

Jason turned on his suit lights and carefully stepped farther into what was obviously a very large airlock. A few more steps and he reached the inner hatch. Jason put out his hand against the partially open hatch and pushed. The hatch swung open easily with no noise. The silence was eerie. However, they were in a vacuum, and it was to be expected.

"Do you see anything?" Greg asked from where he was standing directly behind Jason.

Jason cautiously stepped out into the corridor and slowly turned to look both ways. He could see a closed hatch toward what would be the front of the ship. In the other direction, he could see what looked like several large metal beams and tangled wreckage blocking the corridor. Looking back toward the closed hatch, he could see what appeared to be several doors or possibly corridors leading off deeper into the ship.

"Not a lot," Jason reported as he walked several feet down the corridor in the direction of the closed hatch.

Greg stepped into the corridor and looked around. He felt a little lightheaded as he realized that he was inside an alien spaceship. The corridor was about twelve feet high and nearly ten feet wide. The only light was coming from the bright lights on their spacesuits. He recalled several of the horror movies he had seen as a kid about what could happen on alien spacecraft. He felt the hair on the back of his neck stand up. Those old movies never ended well. He took several deep breaths and calmed back down. He wasn't a kid anymore.

"Let's go down this corridor and check some of those other doors," suggested Jason, gesturing toward the sealed hatch in the distance. "I want to at least go to that hatch and see if it will open."

Greg followed Jason slowly down the corridor. Reaching the first doorway, they found the heavy metal door fully open, exposing the contents of the room. Looking inside, Jason saw several large pieces of strange equipment against the walls. The equipment was covered with numerous dials and switches and what looked like some type of computer screens. All the computer screens looked to be busted, probably from the impact of the crash.

"Nothing much in here," commented Greg, trying to imagine the type of beings that might have once worked in this room. He also was relieved to see that there were no bodies.

"Let's go on to the closed hatch," Jason suggested. He was afraid it was going to take them too long to find the transmitter. They only had so much air and power in their suits before they would have to return to the rover.

The two walked down to the sealed hatch and looked down at the large handle in the center. Reaching forward, Jason grasped the handle and pulled. Nothing happened. Jason spent a minute examining the hatch and decided that it did indeed open toward him. This made sense if this was a pressure hatch since there was an airlock behind them. Jason put his hands on the handle again and tried to turn it, but it still refused to budge.

"Let's both try," Greg suggested.

Greg moved up until he was standing next to Jason, put his hands on the large handle, and then they both tried to turn it. Nothing! It didn't budge any at all.

"It's not moving," Greg muttered, disappointed. "Now what do we do?"

Greg suspected the radio transmitter was somewhere on the other side of this hatch. If he wanted to get back home to his wife and son, they had to find a way around it.

Jason stepped back and looked at the large hatch, wondering what to do next. This seemed to be the only viable exit from this corridor. "We have to get through this hatch," he spoke determinedly. Turning to face Greg, he continued. "As much as I hate to say it, we need to return to the rover and go back to the lander. We're going to need a few tools to get in. We also need to find some way to get the rover to the wreck. With its oxygen recycling system, it will give us the time we need to explore this ship. As big as this thing is, it may take us a while to find the transmitter."

"If it's in a part of the ship we can even get to," Greg added worriedly, recalling the tangled wreckage at the other end of the corridor.

He knew that if it was in the wrecked section, they might not be able to get to it. Their faint hope of being rescued would be dashed. Greg tried not to think about what that would mean. He had a wife and infant son to get back to down on Earth.

The two turned and made their way back down the corridor to the airlock. They walked most of the way in silence. They had a long trip ahead of them back to the lunar lander.

The next day, they were back at the obstructing hatch. They had gotten a good night's rest and loaded up what tools they had available to them on the rover. Jason had spent some time examining the maps they had of the lunar surface. He had found what appeared to be a lower section of the ridge. If the map was correct, they should be able to cross the ridge safely in that location. It had taken an extra two hours, but the rover was now parked next to the open airlock.

They had brought with them a small mallet and what looked like a short piece of metal pipe. They had found the four-foot length of pipe in the wreckage scattered about the ship.

Using the pipe as a lever, Jason and Greg tried to force the hatch handle to move. At first it resisted, then it moved an inch.

"It's moving," Greg grunted as he put even more effort into forcing the hatch handle to open. For another moment, it refused to move, and then the handle suddenly seemed to quit resisting and turned all the way.

"That's it," Jason spoke as he slowly pulled on the handle and the hatch began to open.

Jason pulled the hatch completely open until it touched the corridor wall. They had brought a powerful portable light with them from the lander. Jason shined the light down the corridor. There was another metal hatch, but in front of the hatch it looked as if the corridor turned and went deeper into the ship.

Stepping through the now open hatch, the two slowly walked down the corridor. Occasionally they would stop and glance into rooms with open doors. There were several doors, which were still shut and wouldn't open. Inside the rooms with open doors, more mysterious equipment and even large crates were visible. In every room, there were signs of damage. There was equipment broken loose from the walls, shattered computer screens, even some evidence of fires.

"At least we haven't found any bodies yet," Greg muttered as they went deeper into the ship.

Occasionally Jason would stop and mark the metal wall. He was using a rock they had found on the lunar surface to place an x and an arrow indicating the way back out. They had found several more hatches but so far, all had been open.

"What does this remind you of?" asked Greg, coming to a stop at a flight of stairs that led upward. Something had been haunting the back of his mind for several minutes now. The stairs looked like something you would find on a modern naval ship.

"A navy ship," replied Jason, looking in surprise at the stairs. "To be more precise, a navy warship."

"Exactly," responded Greg, nodding his head. "All those indentations and small hatches in the outer hull, I bet there are weapon emplacements behind them. That's why the hull is so thick and there are so many pressure hatches in the corridors. This is a ship of war!"

Jason was silent for a long moment. He realized that Greg might be right. If he was, then what did that mean for Earth? The universe might be a much more dangerous place than one might have imagined.

"Whoever manned this ship was human like in size," commented Jason pointing at the stairs. "They must have been very similar to us."

"That's comforting to know," Greg replied. He still hoped they didn't come across any alien bodies.

Jason stood for a moment at the base of the stairs. He put one foot cautiously on the first step. "Let's go up to the next level. We need to find the Command Center."

They carefully climbed to the next level. It was not an easy job in their bulky spacesuits. Reaching it, they found several more large, open hatches in front of them.

Something on the wall drew his attention. Looking closer, Jason saw what looked like writing. Walking over to it, he looked in amazement at a map of the ship. There were several maps displayed. On the first map, there was a round dot in a corridor. Jason guessed this was an indication of their current position. The next two maps were for the levels directly above them. Looking carefully at all three maps, he saw nothing that indicated a Command Center or a communications center. He wasn't sure he would recognize such if he saw it.

"We need to go up higher," Jason reported after studying the maps for another moment. Jason could see another set of stairs a little bit farther down the corridor they were now in.

For the next thirty minutes, they continued to climb up into the heart of the ship. They were encountering less damage as they moved closer to the center.

"If this is a ship of war, the Command Center would be located in the most protected spot," Greg pointed out as they finished climbing another set of stairs.

"The center," Jason responded. He had been thinking about that possibility himself. Jason stopped and looked at the three new maps on the wall. On the second map, everything seemed to lead to one general area.

"This might be it," spoke Jason, putting his gloved finger on the spot.

Jason sure hoped it was for Greg's sake. He had promised his friend he would get him home. Only by finding and shutting down that transmitter was it possible. The front section of this ship was so large it would take days for them to search it. Having to drive back and forth from the lunar lander to the wreck would make that almost impossible.

Climbing up to the next level, Jason checked the map and then indicated for Greg to follow him. They were both becoming tired from their exertions. Following the corridor, they finally came to a large sealed hatch.

"Is this it?" asked Greg, breathing heavily.

"I think so," replied Jason, putting his hand on the handle and praying that it would open.

Jason grasped the handle firmly and turned. Much to his surprise it turned easily, and the massive hatch swung inward. This hatch was twice as thick as the others.

"Said the spider to the fly," Greg mumbled over his suit radio.

"If there were any spiders here, they're long dead," Jason responded as he stepped inside and shined his light around.

The room he was in was obviously a Command Center of some kind. The walls were covered with instruments and viewscreens. There were consoles with chairs in front of them. In the center of the room was an upraised console, where possibly the ship's commander and his second in command would have sat.

"This is it!" Greg said excitedly, looking around. "The transmitter has to be here somewhere!"

"Turn your suit lights off," Jason ordered. He turned his off as well as the portable light.

Greg did as ordered and looked around the darkened room. There were numerous dim lights glowing feebly on several consoles.

Neither of the two noticed that behind them, the massive hatch they had just come through slowly swung shut and sealed itself. A sensor in the Command Center had detected human life forms. Following an ancient program, it slowly began activating the ship's AI.

Jason turned his light back on and slowly swung it around the room. He froze when he saw the hatch behind them was closed.

"How did that happen?" Greg asked, bewildered. If neither Jason nor he had shut the hatch, then how the hell was it now closed?

Jason suddenly had the creepy feeling that they were no longer alone in the ship. He stepped back over to the hatch and was about to grasp the handle when the lights in the Command Center began to blink on, one by one. He stopped in mid motion and turned back around.

"What's going on?" asked Greg, suddenly wishing he were back at the rover. He was beginning to feel as if he was in one of those old science fiction horror movies.

"I don't know," replied Jason, thinking furiously. "We must have activated something when we opened the hatch to the Command Center."

A light began flashing on Greg's wrist where a small sensor pad was located. It was used to show breathable atmosphere in the airlock of the lunar lander. "Jason, I'm showing a breathable atmosphere in here now."

"What, that's impossible!" exclaimed Jason, walking over and looking at the sensor on Greg's wrist.

"Nevertheless, it's true," replied Greg, looking around the Command Center nervously. He had a sinking feeling that they were no longer in control of the situation. All they needed now was for one of the alien crew to make an appearance.

Jason stood perfectly still for a moment and then reached a decision. He slowly reached for the hasps that would allow him to remove his helmet.

"Jason, what are you doing?" spoke Greg, frantically realizing what Jason intended.

"I'm taking my helmet off," Jason responded as his hands found the two outer clasps and popped them open.

Once they were unfastened, there was one more inner hasp he had to undo. Hesitantly, he reached for it and slowly popped it open. Then, taking his helmet with both hands, he twisted it and it came loose. Jason tensed, then relaxed as nothing happened. He slowly took his helmet off and stood in the alien Command Center, breathing the air. It was a little cold in the room, but other than that, the air seemed just fine.

"Are you okay?" Greg asked with concern in his voice. He couldn't believe that Jason had risked his life like that. He didn't know what he would have done if something had happened to Jason.

"Yes, I'm fine," replied Jason, taking a deep breath. The air seemed fresh and perfectly normal.

"Well, I guess we know now that these aliens breathed an Earth normal atmosphere," Greg stated as he began reaching for his own helmet fastenings.

Jason stepped over and helped him. Soon both of them had their helmets off. They both turned off their suits' air to conserve it. They would need it later when they left the Command Center, assuming they could find some way out. Right now, the internal atmosphere would be holding the hatch securely shut. For the moment, they were trapped inside this room.

Jason saw another open door on the far side of the Command Center. He walked over toward it and glanced curiously inside. He froze at the sight in front of him. "Greg, you need to come over here! You have to see this!"

Greg came over and stood next to Jason looking into the small room. It looked like a small office with a large desk on the far side. However, what was shocking was what was sitting in the large, comfortable chair behind the desk.

"That's a human!" Greg cried in shock. "How is that possible?"

Jason gazed at the body sitting in the chair. It was mummified, but there was no doubt that it was indeed a human. "It must be the ship's commander," Jason guessed. "We haven't seen any other bodies anywhere. I would guess there was indeed a rescue mission that found the ship. They left the commander here for some reason." Jason reached out and pulled the open door closed behind them. The commander of the ship could rest in peace. They were not going to bother him.

"Sprk, crackle, cmdr, crackle, Earth," suddenly came from a speaker somewhere in the Command Center. "Human, crackle, recu, here," the strange voice continued.

"What is that?" asked Greg, looking around trying to find where the voice was coming from. It sounded artificial, like one of the voice programs on a computer or phone. He wondered what else they had activated by coming into the Command Center.

"I am crackle, ship's compteer," the voice said unclearly.

"We need to talk more," Jason said in sudden understanding. "I think it's trying to learn our language."

For the next fifteen minutes, Jason and Greg talked about everything they could think of. They even walked around the room pointing to different objects and speaking their Earth names.

Then suddenly, for the first time, the voice spoke clearly.

"Ship's status report follows.

Life support operational in Command Center only.

Sublight drive is offline.

FTL drive is off line.

Weapon systems are offline.

Long-range communications are offline.

Emergency beacon has been activated.

Main power sources are offline.

Emergency power is at .05 percent."

"Stop," ordered Jason, hoping the computer would obey him.

"Ship's status report stopped," the voice replied obediently.

"Emergency beacon," repeated Greg, looking over at Jason with renewed hope in his eyes. "That's what we want to turn off. It must be the source of the interference."

"Computer, turn off the emergency beacon," Jason ordered. He waited for a moment, but all that met his ears was silence. He looked over at Greg and then tried again. "Computer, turn off the emergency beacon."

"Emergency beacon will not turn off," the voice replied. "Damaged circuits are not allowing the necessary commands to reach the beacon."

"Crap," Greg muttered. "Now what do we do?"

"Computer, where is the emergency beacon located?" asked Jason, wondering about their next move. The logical thing would be to locate the emergency beacon and turn it off manually.

"Deck seven, section four, communications room two," the voice responded. "There is currently no viable access available to this area due to structural damage to the ship."

"What about from outside the ship?" Jason asked. If they could find a hatch close enough to the damaged area, perhaps they could gain access that way.

"All access hatches have been sealed in that area and will not open due to a lack of power," the voice responded.

"Now what?" Greg asked worriedly. It sounded as if they couldn't get to the beacon to shut it off.

Jason stood next to the command console, thinking. They had come all this way, found an alien or human spaceship, and now were at an impasse because there was no way to shut down the beacon. He just felt as if he was missing something. However, what it was he couldn't quite pin down. It seemed to be just at the edge of his mind.

"I don't know," replied Jason, looking around the room. "There has to be some way to shut that beacon down."

Jason and Greg spent several minutes walking around the Command Center, examining the various consoles. They found navigation, propulsion, weapons, sensors, and various other stations they asked the computer to identify. They found nothing that would help them to shut the emergency beacon down.

Jason asked the computer about the weapons the ship was armed with but was told in a polite voice that he didn't have the proper security clearance to access those files.

"Computer, why are you responding to my voice commands?" Jason asked.

"You are human," the computer replied.

"Was your crew completely human?" Jason asked.

"Yes, this was a human ship."

"Where did this ship come from?" continued Jason, seeking more information.

"That information is classified," the computer responded.

"I still don't see any way to reach that beacon," Greg stated, unhappily. If they could shut down the beacon, they could use the radio on the rover to contact their orbiting command module and speak to Mission Control on Earth.

"There has to be a way," replied Jason, feeling angry with himself and refusing to give up. What was he missing? He knew that there had to be a way.

"We're going to have to start back shortly," Greg said, glancing down at the power reading on his suit. "It took us quite some time to get to the Command Center, and we have just enough power to get back to the rover with some still in reserve."

Jason stared at Greg, wide eyed in astonishment. How could he have overlooked the obvious? "Computer," he said quickly. "What is the ship's current power level?"

"Emergency power is at .045 percent," the voice replied.

Greg looked back at Jason with renewed excitement in his eyes. "Power," he said excitedly. "It's almost out of power."

"How long until all power is exhausted and the emergency beacon shuts down?" Jason asked.

"Four hours and twenty-two minutes at current power usage," the voice responded.

Turning to Greg, Jason smiled. "I think it's time for us to return to the rover. Once the power fails and the beacon stops, we can contact Mission Control through the command module."

"We're going to survive then?" Greg asked. He realized with immense relief that he would indeed get to see his wife and son again. It might just take a while.

"I think so," Jason responded. He then turned and faced the console where the computer voice had been coming from. "Maintain current power usage until the emergency beacon shuts off."

"Affirmative," the voice answered. "Power levels will be maintained until emergency power is depleted."

Jason and Greg helped each other put their spacesuit helmets back on. The air in the room was pumped out and the hatch swung open. Carefully following their marked path, they retraced their steps until they found themselves back at the large hatch. Stepping back outside, they walked over to the waiting rover.

They both sat down in the rover and hooked their suits up to the rover's air and power systems. Now they just had to wait until the interference disappeared from their radio receiver. Once it was clear, they could send a message back to Earth. For several minutes, both men sat staring at the massive spaceship that lay against the crater wall in front of them.

"How do we tell the people back on Earth what we have found?" asked Greg, gazing at the ship in awe. It was hard to imagine something this large flying in space, much less between the stars.

"I don't think we say anything until we get back to Earth," replied Jason, thinking about all the ramifications of their discovery. This would turn the scientific world upside down. "This discovery has the possibility of advancing the human race hundreds of years in a relatively short time."

"It will have to be shared," Greg responded. Their find was going to shake a lot of things up down on Earth. "This discovery is too big for any single country."

The hours passed quickly, and then suddenly the static on the radio receiver vanished. For the first time in several days, the radio was clear of the ever-present static that had been with them since they started their ill-fated descent to the lunar surface.

"The static's gone," Greg said with relief in his voice. The power in the ship had been exhausted.

Reaching forward, Jason set the radio to transmit and took a deep breath. His signal would be relayed by the command module to Earth.

"This is lunar mission New Beginning to Mission Control. Do you read? Over." Jason repeated the message several times and then waited, hoping for a response.

Down on Earth, Elizabeth Johnson was in Mission Control holding her infant son. She was sitting in the observation room gently rocking her baby. For several days now, she had stayed in Mission Control waiting for word on her husband Greg. Her brother's wife sat next to her and was helping to take care of the baby. She had slept very little and had spent a lot of time praying for the safe return of her husband. Commander Strong's sister had just stepped out to get them something to drink.

They both looked up startled when screams and yells of excitement suddenly erupted from the men and women in Mission Control. The director of Mission Control, Tom Hays, turned and sprinted toward the observation room, then swung the door open.

"They're okay!" he said excitedly, his eyes glowing. "We have Commander Strong on the communications channel!"

Elizabeth looked at her sister and started crying tears of joy. Then she looked down at her infant son. His father was okay.

"Where's Katherine?" Tom asked excitedly. He couldn't wait to tell Jason's sister that her brother was on the communications channel.

"She stepped out for a moment," Elizabeth's sister replied. "I'll go get her."

-

Jason and Greg were back in the lunar lander. They now had continuous communication with Mission Control. Jason had spent over an hour explaining the current predicament they were in with the lunar lander. Several mission specialists had been called in to evaluate the dire situation.

"We are going to spend some time evaluating your situation, Jason," Tom said over the radio. "For the time being, we want you to get some rest. We will contact you as soon as we know something."

"Confirmed, Mission Control," replied Jason, shutting down the transmitter.

"They didn't ask about the interference," Greg commented with a puzzled look upon his face. "I wonder why?"

"They had to have picked it up," Jason responded. He also had wondered why they hadn't asked about it. "I don't want to say anything unless they bring it up first."

"So what now?" Greg asked. Tom had arranged for him to talk briefly with his wife. Greg felt as if an immense load had been lifted off his shoulders. Jason had also talked briefly with his sister. Greg was relieved that everyone knew they were safe.

"Let's get some sleep," suggested Jason, feeling exhausted from the day's events. Tom had promised to get word to Jason's brother that he was safe. He knew his sister was relieved. He also knew he was going to hear about this when he got back home.

-

When their sleep period was over, Tom contacted them again.

"It's the opinion of the experts that it's not worth the risk to try to set the lunar lander back upright. The risks of more damage, or even a hull rupture, are too great."

"Then what's the plan?" Jason asked.

He had been afraid it would be impractical to try to put the lunar lander back in an upright position. It was beginning to sound as if they were going to be stranded on the Moon for quite some time.

"We can launch several supply drones to the Moon," Tom replied in a calm voice. "Both can be landed close to your current position. However, it will take us nearly two weeks to get them ready. They're going to have to go through a lot of modifications."

Jason looked inquiringly over at Greg. That would be putting them right on the edge of their food and water supply. It would take some tight rationing.

"We can do it but just barely," replied Greg, doing some quick calculating.

"Affirmative, Mission Control," Jason responded. Then, after thinking for a moment, he continued. "We have some special equipment we would like to request. It looks as if we're going to be stranded here for quite some time."

"At least four months," Tom said. "It will take that long to get another lunar lander ready that we can land and then get it back up safely to the command module."

Jason and Greg looked at each other and then looked around the inside of the cramped lunar lander. Four months in here was going to seem like an eternity.

"We understand," Jason responded. "That's why we're requesting some special equipment so we can get by until then."

"We will do what we can to accommodate you," Tom replied. "Just remember, we only have so much room on the two supply drones."

"We understand, Mission Control," Jason replied. "We will get back to you shortly."

"What kind of supplies did you have in mind?" Greg asked curiously. There just wasn't much room in the lander to store too much more.

"The wrecked spacecraft has a number of compartments that are airtight. Particularly the Command Center and the immediate area around it. If we had a proper power source, some oxygen containers, and another air recycler, we could repressurize part of it. Even if it's just the Command Center, we would have a lot more room than the lander. It would also give us an opportunity to explore that wreck. That would give us something to do for the next four months."

Greg was quiet as he considered the possibility. "If we had the right equipment we could learn a lot. It would definitely be a lot better than sitting around inside this lander for four months."

"Then let's work on a supply list," Jason suggested. "I think Tom already suspects something isn't right. When he sees the list of supplies we're requesting, he is probably going to suspect that we have found something significant. If they know about the interference, which I suspect they do, it won't be too hard for them to put two and two together."

For the next several hours, they put together a list of supplies they would need. They were figuring on one drone for basic supplies such as oxygen, food, water, clothes, and other necessities. The second drone was all supplies to explore the crashed ship with.

When they were through with their list, Jason contacted Mission Control once more. He waited as Tom was summoned and they began going over the list. When Tom heard what they were requesting for the second drone, he became very quiet.

"We will do as you ask," he said finally. "I think I comprehend the importance of all this equipment. It sounds as if you want to set up a habitat away from the lander. I can understand you and Greg not wanting to stay in those cramped quarters for four months. There are a few more things you have not thought of that we will include to help. Is there anything else?"

"Not at the moment," Jason replied. "We will let you know if we think of something."

"What do you think?" Greg asked after they finished talking to Mission Control.

"Tom obviously suspects we have found something," Jason replied. "I felt that when I was talking to him."

"Then I guess now all we have to do is wait," commented Greg, glancing around the small confines of the lander. "I wish I had brought a deck of cards."

Jason smiled and reached down into a small compartment next to his seat. He had a few personal items stored there. He pulled out an unopened deck of playing cards. "Poker?" he asked, gazing innocently at Greg.

"Sure," Greg replied with a smile. Maybe these next two weeks wouldn't be so bad after all.

Two weeks later, they watched as the first drone slowly descended and landed a little over one-mile from the lander. A short time later, the second drone also landed but in the opposite direction. They had instructions to go immediately to the first drone.

Using the lunar rover, they reached the first drone and quickly opened it. Inside the small cargo compartment were numerous small containers and cylinders. The cylinders obviously contained oxygen. The rest of the containers were all labeled with a list of their contents.

It took them three trips to bring everything to the lunar lander. Once at the lander, they moved several of the containers inside. There was one small container about the size of a briefcase that was labeled open first.

Once safely inside the lander, Jason opened the small container. The container held the latest laptop with expanded memory and graphics and a folder marked "Urgent Read First".

Opening the folder, Jason discovered that it contained a long list of possible scenarios that they might have encountered on the Moon.

"This is one hell of a list," Greg commented as they read it. "Everything from competitors from Earth to alien contact. Someone has a really good imagination down there."

"It looks like Tom and his people tried to cover all the bases," Jason replied as he read the list.

There were over two hundred different scenarios listed. Each one had a code at the end that was to be transmitted to Earth. It looked as if the list started with the most likely scenario down to the least likely.

"Here's what we need," Jason said finally. "Wrecked alien spacecraft discovered, no survivors. Code 187ASD."

"What if there had been survivors?" Greg asked thoughtfully.

"Easy," Jason replied. "The one directly below that says wrecked alien spacecraft discovered, alien survivors."

Greg opened another small container he had brought on board. He smiled as he handed Jason a medium sized bulb of drinking water. They each had one and felt much better afterwards. They had been rationing their water very carefully for days.

-

They transmitted the code to Mission Control, knowing it was going to stir up a lot of questions and excitement. For nearly an hour, there was no response. Finally, Tom came back on the radio.

"Jason, we recognize the code. Will you confirm it please?"

Jason retransmitted the code once more. Then they waited.

"Thank you, Jason; you have stirred up quite a ruckus down here. The laptop in the container contains a set of codes we will be using to communicate with from now on. We are also setting up a more secure channel for communication. Activate the laptop and follow the instructions there."

Jason did so. The first thing Greg and he saw was a request for a detailed report of everything that had transpired since they had crashed on the Moon. For nearly four hours, the two worked on the report.

When they felt it was as complete as possible, they hit the transmit icon on the laptop. They had also included their plans to move to the wreck and try to make a small section of it livable.

For nearly eight hours, there was no communication with Earth. Several times Jason was tempted to establish radio contact, but something told him to wait.

"I guess we really stirred up a hornet's nest down there," mumbled Greg, wishing they would hear something. He was also thinking how long four months were going to be without seeing his family.

It was a few minutes later that the laptop chirped, indicating that it was receiving an incoming message. What it said surprised both of them.

"They got the president involved," Greg commented, his eyes widening. That wasn't too surprising. This was something that couldn't be kept away from the government.

"They're going to modify the experimental lander that's still in the test facility," spoke Jason, reading aloud. "They're sending four specialists to aid in our investigation of the wreck. Four weeks until they can get here."

"I guess they're going to strand them here with us," Greg commented. It would be nice to have four more people to talk to. However, this did bring up the question of how Mission Control planned to get all six of them back home.

"They are also sending a lot more equipment and supplies. All of it will be landed in the crater where the crashed ship is. It looks as if they will be launching one supply drone per week once they get started."

"That's one hell of a lot of money someone is shelling out," Greg responded.

Jason leaned back and smiled. "Yes, it is; but look at what we're going to get to do. Just think about what we might learn in the alien ship, especially if we can get the computer working again."

The two took a few moments to think. They would be making history. This was where the human race first made contact with an advanced civilization! The key questions were how was this civilization a human one, and where was it located? The galaxy was a big place. They also wondered what had caused the ship to crash. Had it been in a battle with another spacecraft? There were so many unanswered questions.

Greg opened up another container that had his name on it. Inside were several pictures of his family as well as a private letter from his wife. He gazed for a long moment at the picture of his infant son. Greg looked out one of the viewports in the direction of the crater that contained the wrecked spacecraft. Someday, when his son was old enough, he might travel to the stars. The secret to that was resting in the crater thirty miles distant. Greg leaned back and smiled; the future looked extremely bright.

On the wrecked alien spacecraft, a small dim light was glowing on a console. The ship's AI was fully activated. The AI had carefully watched the two humans in the Command Center. It had made sure the computer listed the remaining power on its list of ship systems. It had wanted to see if these new humans were capable of figuring out how to shut the emergency beacon off. They had passed the test. Now the AI waited. It had its own internal power source. It had much to tell this new human race.

The End

Moon Wreck: Revelations

Chapter One

Jason stood in his spacesuit at the top of the ridge, gazing down at the wrecked spaceship in the crater. It was still difficult to accept that a spaceship manned by humans had crashed here on the Moon many years ago. The main section of the wreck was on the far side of the crater and relatively intact. There were so many unanswered questions. Where had the ship come from? What was it doing here? Why was it manned by humans? What had caused it to crash? Jason took a deep breath and shifted his mind back to the job at hand. Those questions would have to wait for a while.

He was using a special camera sent up by Mission Control to take photos of all the different wreckage scattered across the mile wide crater. The wreckage was covered with lunar dust, and there was a massive amount of wreckage. Jason wondered if there had been an explosion in the ship, which had split it into pieces. Greg was down on the floor of the crater walking from one mangled piece to the next as Jason took the photos. Greg would stop and stand by a piece of wreckage so they would have something to show the comparative sizes of the debris they were taking pictures of.

"I think it's about time to go back in," Greg complained over his suit radio. "I've walked all over this crater today. I didn't realize there was so much wreckage."

Jason laughed and nodded his head in agreement. It had been a long day. "Get over to that next large piece that looks like part of an engine assembly. Once we have that one recorded, we can go in. Mission Control wants images of everything."

Greg trudged over to the indicated piece of wreckage. After reaching it, he turned to face Jason. He could just barely make out Jason's white, spacesuited figure on top of the ridge.

After the last photograph was taken, Greg waited patiently as Jason made his way carefully back down to the floor of the crater. Once the two were together, they turned and started walking toward the large wreck against the crater wall. They had discovered the wrecked human spaceship a little over four weeks ago after their lunar lander had crash-landed on the Moon. The wrecked spaceship had detected their descent and activated an emergency beacon. Its broadcast had disabled all the computer systems in the lander, causing the crash.

"I still can't believe this ship is here," spoke Greg, looking at the looming wreck.

"Well, it is," Jason replied.

It had been a busy four weeks, which had been a good thing. That had helped to take their minds off their families down on Earth. Even so, with everything they were trying to accomplish they still thought about their loved ones, knowing it would be months before they saw them again.

A few minutes later, the two approached the wrecked spaceship. For the last three weeks, the two of them had been photographing and exploring the accessible sections of the wreck. In two more days, the refurbished lunar lander from Earth would be landing with four more explorers. Then all six of them would be stranded on the Moon for at least another three months until a new lander and command module could be made ready for the rescue mission. The U.S. government had stepped in and furnished literally unlimited funding for the current mission and the retrieval. The technology inside the wrecked spaceship had been incentive enough to get the government heavily involved.

They entered the ship through the large airlock they had discovered when they first found the wreck and made their way down several long corridors. They had rigged up some emergency lighting powered by several large solar panels to furnish a dim light in the corridors. The solar panels had been sent up on one of the supply drones after Jason and Greg had reestablished contact with Mission Control.

They reached their destination, which were two small rooms with a portable airlock attached. The airlock had also been sent up on one of the supply drones. After a few minor modifications to the airlock, they had managed to seal off several rooms to live in. The idea of being cooped up in the lunar lander for a number of weeks had been extremely unappealing.

After passing through the airlock, they entered the sealed compartments and began removing their suits. They were in a small, 12 by 14 foot room, with another room of the same size visible through an adjoining door. These two rooms had been their living quarters for the last several weeks.

"Home sweet home!" said Greg as he sat down in a comfortable chair, glad to be able to get off his feet. He reached down and began massaging his right ankle. "Glad we're still not cooped up in the lander."

"I agree," Jason replied as he sat down behind a desk they had managed to carry in. The desk had a laptop and printer on it as well as other documents. There were numerous photos spread out across the desk of some of their more interesting discoveries.

They had found several chairs and other furnishings which they had moved into the rooms to make them more livable. Power for the rooms came from another solar power bank they had set up outside, and a small air recycler kept their air fresh and breathable. A small self contained heating unit kept the rooms warm.

"I want to try to go deeper into the center of the ship tomorrow," said Jason, studying some printouts he had made of their explorations so far. He laid the tip of his finger on a photo. "If we can get through this large sealed door, we should be able to access the center section."

Greg nodded his head in agreement. "I wish we could power up that computer in the Command Center. It's bound to have a lot of stored information we could access. Maybe we could find out what happened to this ship and where it came from."

"I agree," replied Jason, laying down a printout and looking over at Greg. "But we don't dare risk activating the emergency beacon again. One of the people coming up on the lander is a computer expert, and the other two are engineers. Hopefully, they can help us to bypass or turn off the emergency beacon so it won't come back on. Colonel Marten Greene is the pilot, and he has a pretty solid background in communications."

Greg nodded. It had been a good idea to move into the ship. They had managed to explore several areas, but the center section, as well as the weapons areas, were still locked down. They had stayed out of the damaged areas for the time being, not wanting to risk getting trapped by the wreckage. Tomorrow, they would try one more time before the other crew arrived to access the center section.

So far they had found no more bodies in their exploration of the crashed spaceship. It was obvious that all the bodies had been removed except the commander, who was in the small room off the Command

Center. The big question was, had the bodies been removed by a rescue ship or were they waiting for them inside the center section? The more they had explored, the more obvious it became that this was a ship of war. It was heavily armored with numerous bulkheads and hatches. From their explorations outside, they estimated that there were over sixty weapon emplacements behind the sealed hatches. That was assuming that each of the hatches contained weapons.

"Who do you think they were fighting?" asked Greg, picking up and looking at several photographs of the hatches on the outside of the ship.

He could just imagine laser cannons or some type of sophisticated plasma beamers hidden behind the closed hatches. He had watched numerous science fiction shows as a kid, and he knew he was letting his imagination get the best of him. But it was still intriguing to think about.

"It's hard telling," replied Jason, leaning back in his chair and looking over at Greg. "It could have been other humans or even aliens. We won't know until we can access that computer."

"I hope it wasn't aliens, and I hope this crash occurred a long time ago," spoke Gregg, feeling an icy shiver run down his back. That had been his biggest fear when they had first found the ship. Finding alien bodies or even a live alien wasn't on his agenda.

"I just hope we have enough power to activate the computer when the others get here," added Jason, rubbing his forehead with his right hand.

The isolation from their families had been difficult for both of them since the crash. Staying busy had helped, but they couldn't stay busy all the time. There were times when it was difficult not to think about their families down on Earth. Especially when they were done with their explorations for the day and they had a little spare time.

"We have two energy sources that Mission Control has sent up on the most recent supply drones," reported Greg, looking at an inventory sheet, which listed all of the supplies that had been sent up so far. "They seem pretty sure that these will be able to supply the energy needed to power up the computer and the other equipment in the Command Center. They are similar to the RTG power sources of a few years ago. These are supposedly more efficient and don't have the heat problems."

"Have you talked to your wife today?" asked Jason, knowing that Greg was really missing his family.

The truth was they were both missing their families back down on Earth. To communicate with Mission Control they had to go outside and use the radio on the lunar rover, which was parked just outside the large airlock.

"Briefly," responded Greg, feeling the loneliness of being separated from his wife and son. "Elizabeth's doing fine, and I hope to have a longer talk with her tomorrow. She's having a difficult time considering the situation." It had been hard being away from his family for so long. The occasional conversations set up by Mission Control helped. But they were still separated by nearly a quarter of a million miles.

Jason nodded his head in understanding. He had talked to his brother briefly the previous day over a secure com line. His brother had told him there were all kinds of rumors going around about what had happened to the New Beginning's mission. Trevor had also mentioned that their sister Katherine was still highly upset. She had taken it extremely hard when all contact had been lost initially with the lander as it was descending to the Moon. Katherine had camped out in Mission Control until contact had finally been reestablished.

Once he got home, Jason knew he was going to get an earful from his sister. He couldn't blame her. This also wouldn't be the first time. She had been extremely upset when he had volunteered to be a military test pilot. It had put a strain on their relationship for quite some time.

"The last two drones also have a lot of different tools and equipment on board that we may be able to use to get into some of those sealed compartments," Greg continued as he studied the supply list.

They had found numerous compartments that seemed to be locked down and wouldn't open. Greg guessed that the more sensitive and interesting equipment the ship contained were behind those sealed hatches. They had yet to find any power sources or weapons.

"Let's get some rest; we can get a good start in the morning," replied Jason with a yawn.

He would have to go outside in the morning and send the latest photos and a report to Mission Control of their most recent explorations. Their communications didn't work well from inside the ship. The hull was just too thick.

Unknown to either of them, the ship's AI was monitoring their conversations. It was still evaluating these new humans and trying to decide when it should make its presence known. The AI's internal power source was rapidly weakening from its increased use since the humans had arrived. At its current depletion rate, it would be too low to sustain the AI in another two weeks. The AI desperately needed a new power source and that might force it to contact the humans before it was ready.

Early the next morning, Jason and Greg were standing in front of the large hatch, which led to the center section of the ship. The lights from their spacesuits lit up the hatch and the corridor around it. They had walked through a number of dark corridors to reach this point deep inside the ship. Reaching forward, Jason grasped the handle and turned it. Much to his surprise, it turned easily and the hatch swung open.

"What the hell?" exclaimed Greg, looking over at Jason.

Just yesterday morning the handle had refused to budge. They had tried everything they could think of to open it, and it hadn't moved an inch. Now it opened without any use of force at all.

"Well, it's open," commented Jason, shining his lights inside the open hatch. It showed another corridor leading off in opposite directions.

"That's just it. It shouldn't have opened," Greg muttered.

Sometimes he had the eerie feeling that something or someone was watching them. He felt an icy shiver race up his back. That was happening too often recently. Even though this ship had crashed years ago, Greg still found himself jumping at shadows. He didn't believe in ghosts, but sometimes he felt as if there was a presence inside the ship watching their every move. He couldn't explain the feeling; it was just with him constantly.

Jason stepped inside the open hatch and then, as an afterthought, laid a small tool across the hatch wedging it open. Shining the portable light down the corridor, he saw numerous doors, all of which were shut. "Let's check several of these rooms and see what they contain."

Greg walked over to a door and opened it. Shining his light inside, he was surprised to see a small desk, several chairs, and two bunks. The chairs and the desk were heavily damaged from being knocked around. He knew they had probably been damaged as a result of the crash. "These look like crew's quarters."

Jason stepped inside and looked around more closely. Going over to the desk, he set it up and opened one of the drawers. The drawer had a small catch on it that had kept it closed. There were a few papers inside, but he didn't see anything of interest. Looking around, he didn't see any personal items either. He had hoped to find some photos or something that might have given a hint as to the life style of the crew. Most crewmembers on Earth military ships had pictures of their families around somewhere. He didn't see any of that here.

They checked a few more rooms and found them all to be the same. This section must have been where the crew lived. The quarters were small but still spacious by military standards. It was also obvious that everything of a personal nature had been removed.

As they walked down the corridor, Jason placed small magnetic LED lights on the wall every fifty feet or so to furnish some illumination. They would allow them to find their way back more easily, and all you had to do was press their lighted surfaces to turn them off.

For several minutes, they made their way deeper into the heart of the ship. Some of the rooms now contained more sophisticated equipment, much of it damaged or hopelessly smashed. The crash had wrecked almost everything that wasn't anchored down. They stopped and examined some of the equipment, but for the most part it was difficult to tell exactly what it had been used for.

"I'm surprised anything survived intact," Greg commented as he looked into a room containing numerous boxes and crates that were in shambles. These were obviously supplies of some kind. He rummaged through several damaged boxes, finding them all to be empty. Whatever had once been here had been removed.

Going into another corridor, they found another large, sealed hatch in front of them with some sort of writing on it. It didn't look like any form of writing either of them were familiar with. They looked at each other, wondering what could be behind this one.

"That looks like a warning of some kind," Greg said uneasily as his eyes studied the strange letters.

"It could be," replied Jason, wondering if they should attempt to open it. "We have come this far; we might as well have a look."

Most of the hatches had some type of writing on them. On this one, the writing was much larger. In Greg's mind, he could hear his wife saying, "Don't go in there!". She had always been the cautious type. Just thinking about her made Greg wish that he could see her and their newborn son; he really missed them. But that was at least another three months in the future. He let out a deep breath and turned his attention back to the hatch.

Jason hesitated for a moment. Greg was right; there was something about this hatch that didn't feel right. Fortifying himself, he reached out and turned the handle. He had to use a little more force than he expected, and then the door swung open. Stepping inside, he froze when brilliant lights flashed on, illuminating the entire area.

"Lights!" exclaimed Greg, his eyes opening wide. How was that possible?

"Emergency lighting," responded Jason, studying the lights on the wall. "Probably battery powered, and they turned on when we activated a hidden sensor as we stepped in here. I doubt whether they will last long. Over the years, most of their charge has probably bled off."

Jason turned his own lights off and noticed what looked like long glass windows that stretched along both sides of the corridor. This had to be some type of heavy-duty safety glass to have survived the crash. He walked up curiously to one of the windows and looked in. He stepped back, shocked at what was on the other side. "We just found the rest of the crew!"

"What?" responded Greg, walking over and looking inside the brightly lit room. He shuddered involuntarily at what he saw inside.

There were dozens of beds with crewmembers laid out. Someone had taken the time after the wreck to bring the dead crew down here for their final resting place. He wondered if it had been the commander. Going over to the other window on the opposite side, Greg saw the same thing. There must be over a hundred bodies laid out.

"This looks more like a hospital," spoke Jason, taking out his camera and photographing what they were seeing. It looked as if there were monitoring equipment and other specialized medical devices against the walls.

"Jason," Greg said quietly as he studied the inside of the room behind the glass, "I don't think these people all died from the crash. Some of them don't look to be that injured."

Studying the men and women in the room, Jason realized that Greg was right. "A disease?" Jason asked.

"That would be my guess," responded Greg, turning around to face Jason. "I don't think we want to open any of these doors. Whatever killed these people should be gone by now due to the extreme cold. Colonel Greene, the pilot flying the specialists up, has some medical experience. Perhaps he can give us a better idea as to what happened here."

Jason took a deep breath. It seemed that everywhere they went in the ship they found more mysteries and unanswered questions. If they could get the ship's computer back up and running, once the specialists arrived perhaps they could find out what had happened.

Let's go back," spoke Jason, stepping back away from the glass and turning to face Gregg. "We'll come back when the others get here."

"Sound fine to me," replied Greg, looking at the lighted rooms. The emergency lighting was already starting to dim. "This ship is spooky enough. Now we have all these dead bodies."

The two started back down the corridor, shutting the hatches behind them and retracing their steps by following the LED lights they had placed on the walls. They would write their report up and then wait for tomorrow. The inbound lunar lander would be arriving and Jason and Greg had a lot to show the four new explorers.

—

Jason and Greg were outside in the rover watching the space above them expectantly. A bright light suddenly appeared amongst the stars and began to descend toward them.

"There they are," Greg said excitedly, pointing upward. With his eyes locked on the descending lander, Greg took a deep, steadying breath.

"This is Rescue One to New Beginnings," a friendly voice came over the com channel. "We have begun our descent and should be with you shortly."

"We read you," Jason replied evenly. "We are standing by in the rover."

"It's going to feel good to see some new faces," Greg commented, his eyes still focused on the descending lunar lander. He felt growing excitement knowing that shortly they wouldn't be alone on the Moon.

"Tired of looking at me," joked Jason, smiling.

He knew how Greg felt. New faces and new voices would help break the monotony. Greg and he were running out of things to talk about, other than the wreck. Four weeks was a long time to be stranded together in small quarters.

"Once they get here we can really begin exploring the ship," Greg spoke, elatedly. "We can get the computer powered back up and maybe get some of those other sealed doors open. I really want to see what's behind those sealed hatches on the ship's hull.'"

"So does the government," responded Jason, recalling a recent conversation with Tom Hays, the mission controller back down on Earth.

For several minutes, they watched the new lander descend, until it finally landed nearly half a mile away from them in a level and debris free section of the crater. They watched as its engines shut off and the dust began to settle back down. Once everything seemed clear, Jason started the rover toward the landing site.

"Their touchdown went smooth," commented Greg, sounding pleased and relieved. It had been one of his worst nightmares that the emergency beacon would come back on and sabotage the landing.

"Their computers and other vital equipment are shielded," responded Jason, maneuvering the rover around several small pieces of wreckage. "We weren't going to take a chance on anything happening to this lander."

It only took a few minutes to reach the landing site. As they pulled up, the hatch to the lander was already opening. An astronaut appeared and, looking around, waved at Jason and Greg.

"Commander Strong, it's good to be here!"

"Glad you could join us, Colonel Greene," responded Jason, climbing out of the rover. "That was a textbook landing."

"Computers handled it," Greene confessed as he stepped down onto the lunar surface. "We have some supplies to unload, as well as another rover we need to get down."

Looking up, Jason saw another astronaut step out of the lander and begin their descent to the lunar surface. "Let's get to it," Jason responded.

Chapter Two

Four hours later, all six of them were in the quarters that Jason and Greg had put together. They had made several trips between the lander and the wrecked spaceship. All the supplies were stacked in the corridor outside. Along with Colonel Greene, there were engineering specialists Adam Simmins, Marcus Edwards, and computer specialist Lisa Gordon.

"I must say, I'm impressed," commented Greene, looking around the two rooms. "This is definitely better than staying in the lander."

"It's nice just to be able to stretch," commented Lisa, brushing a lock of blonde hair out of her eyes.

She was glad she had brought some regular clothes besides her blue flight uniform. There wouldn't be a lot of privacy in these two rooms, but she had been prepared for that when she had volunteered for this mission. It was still a lot better than sleeping in the lander.

"We have several supply drones that we need to unload, as well as the rest of the supplies from your lander," commented Greg realizing that both Jason and he probably could use a shower.

He was extremely conscious of the fact that their quarters didn't smell all that great. With the new supplies, they could at least take a sponge bath. It was not his favorite way to take a bath, but it was better than nothing. They had water, but they had been conserving it since they had no way to recycle it.

Lisa continued to look around, recognizing that these quarters could certainly use a woman's delicate touch. But for now she was more interested in seeing the computer and the control systems in the command center. That was why she had come. "How soon can we go to the Command Center? I would like to see the computer and the other control systems."

"I suggest we spend the rest of the day getting all the supplies inside, then early tomorrow we can check out the Command Center and some of the other areas," Colonel Greene commented. He had spent quite a bit of time talking to Tom Hays back in Mission Control. "We may need some of those supplies for our exploration of this ship."

"I agree with that," added Jason, nodding his head. "Once we have all the supplies inside we can concentrate on exploring the ship."

Turning toward Jason, Colonel Greene continued. "From your reports and the images you have sent back, the ship's Command Center seems to be pretty much intact. As soon as Lisa, Adam, and Marcus feel it's safe we will attach one of the RTGs to the computer system and see if we can power it back up."

"That might reinitiate the emergency beacon," Jason warned, his eyes narrowing.

There were still some supply drones on the schedule that would be landing over the next several weeks. He didn't want to cause them to crash. They would need those supplies. That damn beacon had already caused enough problems.

"I'm not too worried about that," replied Greene, folding his arms across his chest. "We have the equipment to get into the section the beacon's located in if necessary. The equipment is still on the lander. Unless these bulkheads are much tougher than they look, we should be able to cut through them."

"This is a warship," Jason reminded Colonel Greene. "I suspect those bulkheads are a lot tougher than you think."

Greene was silent for a moment, and then replied. "We can always take the power away and silence it like you did the first time."

"We also need to look for a larger area to attach a portable airlock," added Adam Simmins, looking around critically and noticing the size of the two rooms. "A lot of the equipment we brought needs to be inside where we can access it easily. It's going to become crowded in here rather quickly."

"I don't see a problem with that," Jason replied in agreement. Six people in these quarters plus equipment and the lander might seem roomy. "There are some larger interconnected rooms farther down the corridor that we could use. We would have to move some equipment and other stuff out, but I think we could make them livable."

"That would work," spoke Simmins, pleased at the thought of having even more room to live and work in.

"However, I suggest we get the computer activated first," continued Jason, thinking about the possibilities. "It controls the ship's environmental systems, and we know they still work since the computer pressurized the Command Center when we first went in there. We might be able to use the computer to pressurize some other compartments that would be more comfortable."

"Sounds like a plan," replied Lisa, anxious to get to the computer. "I'm curious to see just how this computer is programmed and the differences between it and our own operating systems."

"Be patient, Lisa," Colonel Greene said, smiling. He well understood the young woman's desire to see the Command Center and the computer; he wanted to see it also. But they had other work to do first.

"Let's take an hour to relax and then we'll start moving the rest of the equipment and supplies," ordered Greene, wanting to get started as soon as possible. "With two rovers it shouldn't take us too long."

Two hours later, Jason and Greg were on the far side of the crater where one of the drones had landed several days previously. The small drone was basically a small cargo pod with an engine and four short landing struts. The landing didn't have to be perfect as long as the drone got down relatively undamaged. The drone sat at a slight angle with a bent strut. Burn marks beneath marked where the descent engine had fired.

Greg looked around the desolate landscape of the crater. Even from here, the wrecked spaceship was imposing. It lay smashed against one rim of the crater. He wondered how much farther it would have slid if the crater wall hadn't stopped it. There was a thin layer of lunar dust on everything. That was one thing Greg hated about the Moon, all the damn dust. It got into everything.

Greg kicked the dust with one of his spacesuit's boots and frowned, watching it fly up. Just walking sent up little puffs of dust at times. "I hate this dust," muttered Gregg, looking at the drone.

Jason stood next to the drone. Reaching up, he grasped a latch on the hatch and turned. He followed the same procedure for the other three latches. In moments, he had the small hatch open and, reaching inside, began taking out the small bundles of supplies that were stored inside. More food, water, and other basics they might need. It would take two trips with the rover to get everything back to the wreck. Looking up, Jason stared at the Earth. The friendly blue and white globe made him feel homesick for his sister and brother. All his life, the three of them had always been there for each other. Due to the security slapped on the current mission, his conversations with his siblings the last few days had been brief.

"Let's get this unloaded," said Jason, turning to Greg. "We have a lot to do."

The next day, they were all in the Command Center. Lisa was examining the computer and had a panel off one side so she could see the processors. The two engineers were tracing wiring and checking for obvious damage.

"This doesn't look too different from our own computers," Lisa commented in surprise, shining a bright light inside the console. She turned her deep blue eyes toward Colonel Greene. "There are a few things different internally, but it's still just a basic computer."

"I would have thought it would be far more advanced," commented Greene, frowning. "These people seem so far ahead of us technically that I assumed their computers would be also."

"Is it safe to turn back on?" asked Jason, walking over to stand next to Lisa. He was still nervous about the possibility of reactivating the emergency beacon.

"As soon as I get this panel back on, it shouldn't be a problem," replied Lisa, standing back up and wishing she could stretch decently. It wasn't easy to bend over in a cumbersome spacesuit. "We just need to get some power to it."

"What about the power?" asked Greene looking over at the two engineers who had several panels off one wall, examining the wiring behind it.

"No problem," responded Adam, turning to face the colonel. "We've located the main power lead, and all we have to do is attach the RTG to it."

"What do you think, Commander Strong?" asked Greene, turning toward Jason.

"Let's do it," Jason replied with a nod. "We have a lot of unanswered questions and that computer could hold the keys. As you said, we can always cut the power."

"Very well, let's get the power hooked up."

Power, the AI thought as it watched the humans in the Command Center. It could siphon off power from the human's power source to replenish its own diminishing power reserves. This would solve the immediate power problem and give the AI more time to observe these new humans. The AI watched with interest as two of the humans attached their power source to the main power conduit for the Command Center. The AI made a few quick adjustments to some of the systems to ensure that all the power went to the systems in the

Command Center and didn't bleed back out into damaged lines and consoles in other sections of the ship. Its own power levels were getting dangerously low.

"RTG is hooked up," reported Adam Simmins, stepping back from where he had been working and watching it. Trying to get everything attached properly while wearing a bulky spacesuit was a challenge. The RTG was a round cylinder approximately four feet tall and two feet in diameter.

"Turn it on," ordered Colonel Greene, taking a deep breath. "I want everyone to watch the consoles and see if anything happens. Adam, if I tell you to cut the power I want it off instantly!"

Simmins nodded and reached over and flipped a switch. Instantly, several lights on the RTG blinked on. Other than that, nothing seemed to happen.

"The computer's not coming on," reported Lisa, gazing at the screen and wondering if there was a button she needed to push. She felt disappointed that the computer hadn't reacted to the power being restored.

"It may be necessary to let the power build up," suggested Jason looking around the Command Center. "There may be some type of minimum power requirement for the Command Center in order for its systems to function."

He had at least expected a few lights or something to come on when the RTG had been activated. No lights had come on or anything. All the consoles were still dark. Everything was eerily still. Jason felt a little uneasy that nothing had come on. Something just didn't feel right. Where was the power going?

For two hours, Jason watched power flow into the systems in the Command Center. While they waited, everyone spent their time examining the consoles and controls. Jason did his best to explain to the others what Greg and he had found out the first time they had talked to the computer. Everyone listened and asked questions. They all felt intrigued by what the computer had said and what it might know.

"This computer seems very advanced in its programming," Lisa commented as she listened to Jason. "The way it reacted to your voice commands indicates a high level of programming."

"I just hope it can answer some of our questions," Greg added. "I have been waiting for weeks to find out where this ship came from."

"We have a lot of questions to ask also," spoke Colonel Greene, recalling everything that Tom Hays and he had discussed. For the time being Washington was leaving Tom Hays in charge of this mission. Tom was well qualified and had worked with Washington before on other missions.

Jason looked speculatively around the Command Center. It was laid out in the shape of a rectangle. There were a dozen control stations along the walls, a command console in the center where the commander would have sat, and a plotting table off to one side of the command console. Jason stood, trying to picture in his mind what this room must have looked like when it was operational and with its crew in place. He found it hard to imagine the sights the crew of this ship must have seen. There were large viewscreens on all four walls, with the largest on the front wall. This room must have been breathtaking when the ship was flying between the stars.

Bringing his mind back to the present, Jason realized there had to be some type of power storage device located somewhere that required a minimum charge before activating any of the Command Center's systems. Simmins and Edwards had checked the RTG and confirmed that it was generating power.

"Nothing wrong here," reported Simmins, standing up and stepping away from the RTG once again. "It's generating plenty of power, but I can't tell you where it's going."

"I would think by now there should be sufficient power to operate the computer," added Edwards, feeling confused. "The power has to be going somewhere."

"This is taking a lot longer than I expected," commented Lisa, walking over and looking at the dark computer console. She was beginning to get impatient. She wanted access to the computer!

The words were hardly out of her mouth when the computer console came on. The screen lit with a faint glow. At the same instant, the hatch to the Command Center suddenly shut. Before Jason could say anything, the overhead lights came dimly on.

"What's happening?" snapped Colonel Greene, realizing they were shut in. He looked over at Jason wanting an answer.

Jason looked at a readout on his suit and saw that the Command Center was being pressurized. "The computer is pressurizing the Command Center."

"Just like it did last time," Greg commented with relief in his voice.

A few moments later, Jason checked the readings once more. Everything seemed normal. Nodding at the others, Jason removed his helmet. The air was fine, even though the room was still cool. The air was being heated, but it would take a few more minutes to be warm enough to feel comfortable.

Greg and Colonel Greene quickly followed suit. When the other three saw that everything seemed to be okay, they removed theirs also.

"Do you think it's safe to take our spacesuits off completely?" asked Lisa, wanting to get her hands on the computer. It was difficult to work in these cumbersome spacesuits.

"It should be," replied Jason nodding. "The computer didn't depressurize the Command Center until we told it to last time."

"The Command Center will stay pressurized," a computer voice suddenly spoke. "Command Center power reserves are at 1 percent and rising. All bulkheads and emergency safety fields are optimal."

Lisa stepped back in surprise, looking at the computer. Evidently, this computer could respond to voice commands as well as respond to what it heard in the Command Center. She recalled reading that in the report that Commander Strong had sent to Mission Control. She just hadn't expected the computer to start talking immediately.

Greg walked over to the computer so he could ask it a question. He had been impatient to find out the answer to one particular question that had been bothering him since they had first found the wreck. "Computer, where did this ship come from?"

"That information is classified," the voice replied.

"Damn, that's what it said last time," Greg moaned in disappointment. He turned to Lisa and frowned. "Getting answers might not be as easy as we had hoped."

"Perhaps you asked the wrong question," spoke Lisa thoughtfully. She had a lot of experience dealing with computers. Oftentimes a question had to be phrased properly to get a response.

"Computer, what was the name of your ship's point of origin?"

"The Human Federation of Worlds," the computer responded promptly.

"And how many systems were in the Federation?" Lisa continued, pleased that the computer had answered her first question.

"That information is classified," the computer replied.

"Was there a war going on?" Jason asked suddenly.

"Yes," responded the computer.

"Who were you fighting?"

"The Hocklyn Empire."

"Were the Hocklyns human?"

"No."

Everyone was stunned as they gazed at each other. The war had been against aliens! This was not what any of them had wanted to hear.

Jason hesitated for a moment trying to decide just how to ask the next question. Evidently the computer would give out information as long as it wasn't too detailed. "What happened to the Human Federation of Worlds?"

The computer was silent for a moment. It wasn't going to answer the question until it was overruled by the watching AI. "The Federation was destroyed."

Everyone in the room became quiet. Somewhere out in the galaxy an alien empire had wiped out a human civilization. A ship from that destroyed civilization had evidently made it to Earth's Moon. The question was, why?

"What happened to the Hocklyns?" asked Colonel Greene, hoping that both sides had managed to wipe each other out. Earth didn't need to get involved with a threat from space.

The AI had now taken over complete control of the computer. It wanted the humans to know what awaited them in their future. Later, when it revealed itself, the AI would give them even more detailed information.

"They still survive. Their empire comprises hundreds, possibly thousands of worlds."

"Thousands," Greene repeated stunned, his eyes widening in concern. He looked around at the others. "How did their empire get so large?"

"The Hocklyns are members of the Slaver Empire, which covers much of the center of the galaxy. Only twelve systems are actually inhabited by the Hocklyns. The other systems were all conquered by them or their allies."

"Their allies?" asked Jason feeling uneasy. "What do you mean, their allies?"

"There are three other races along with the Hocklyns that control the military power of the Slaver Empire. These four races are each responsible for a section of the empire. The Hocklyns were responsible for the section in which the Human Federation of Worlds was located."

"What do the Hocklyns do to the worlds they conquer, and why did they completely destroy the Human Federation of Worlds?" Jason asked, his tone indicting his concern.

They had just found out there were multiple alien worlds and none of them were friendly toward humans. If this Hocklyn Empire was still out there, how long would it be before they found Earth? Jason felt a huge emptiness form in the pit of his stomach. Looking at the others, Jason saw stunned and disbelieving looks upon their faces.

"The Hocklyns conquer a world and then that world works for the Slaver Empire, furnishing whatever material goods the empire requires of it. Conquered worlds are not allowed to have a military, and their populations are strictly controlled."

"What happens if a world refuses to furnish what the Hocklyns demand?" asked Colonel Greene, looking over at Jason worriedly.

"The Hocklyns will make an example of that world so others will not attempt to do the same. They have been known to destroy the largest city on the planet, and then continue to wipe out other cities until the rebelling world capitulates to their demands."

"What about the Human Federation of Worlds? Why were they destroyed and not conquered?" Jason asked. These Hocklyns sounded like a race he never wanted to encounter.

"The Federation chose to fight. We had a powerful fleet and felt it could stand up to the Hocklyns. We were wrong. The Hocklyns made an example of the Federation."

The room was silent for a moment as everyone attempted to digest what the computer was telling them. This story sounded so fantastic! Nevertheless, this ship was a warship, and it was here on the Moon. There was no reason to think the computer was making this up.

"Why is your ship here?" asked Colonel Greene, fearing the answer.

"This was the only other known human world. We came to set up a base and warn your people that the Hocklyns are coming."

The room was quiet, and it suddenly seemed colder. No one noticed that the computer was no longer answering with "this information is classified" any longer. The AI was in full control of the ship's computer.

Jason stared at the computer with a cold chill running down his back. He was picturing his family back on Earth and the threat they might someday face. "When?" he asked.

Upon the front wall of the Command Center, the large viewscreen suddenly came to life. A map of the known galaxy appeared. The center was covered in red and as they watched, the red slowly grew as it spread out across the galaxy. It approached one of the spiral arms where there was a blinking emblem. It slowly reached the blinking emblem, causing it to go out, and then continued on.

Colonel Greene and Jason stepped over close to the screen. There were numbers scrolling across which they suspected represented a timeline.

"At the current rate of expansion, the Hocklyn Empire will reach this solar system in 268 of your years. The Slaver Empire will control the entire galaxy another 1,200 years after that."

Everyone felt relief at the threat not being imminent.

"We have time, then," spoke Colonel Greene, looking at the others. "We have 268 years to get our planet ready."

"What do you mean?" Greg asked, confused. "Ready for what?"

"It means that learning how this ship functions and everything that goes into constructing a warship like this one will have to be researched," Greene replied with dark and determined eyes. From a military standpoint, he understood the threat that the Hocklyns represented to the future of Earth. "This ship just became our planet's greatest asset and perhaps its only hope for survival. If what this computer just told us is true, the Hocklyns are coming and there is nothing we can do to change that."

The five others looked at each other, realizing just what Colonel Greene's words meant. Then they gazed back at the large screen, which showed the red continuing to grow until it covered the entire galaxy. This discovery on the Moon was about to change life on Earth.

Chapter Three

Colonel Greene and Jason were inside one of the medical wards staring at one of the bodies on a table. It appeared to be that of a young man in his late twenties. There was considerable damage done to the body from the cold and airless environment in which it had been kept. Colonel Greene reached forward and pulled the covering completely off.

"Body seems to be completely human," Greene commented as his eyes swept over all the visible parts. "I would need to do a complete autopsy to make sure."

He walked over to several other bodies and, choosing a woman, did the same thing. She looked to be in her early to mid thirties. Everything looked perfectly normal for a human female.

"What do you think killed them?" Jason asked. He could count thirty bodies in this room. Three more rooms besides this one were full of bodies. That made a total of 120. He wondered just how large the ship's crew complement had been?

Greene sighed deeply. This had been troubling him also. Ever since Commander Strong had told him about the dead bodies he had wondered what had happened.

"Some of them may have died in the crash," he responded, taking the coverings off several more bodies. "With the state of the bodies, it's difficult to tell. Out best bet may be to ask the computer."

"I wonder if there's a medical computer in here?" asked Jason, gazing around at all the equipment on the walls. The equipment showed very little damage as it was securely fastened down.

"Probably," replied Greene, taking a moment to look around the room. "Once Lisa gets finished in the Command Center, we may have to bring her down here."

"Have you sent Mission Control your report about the Hocklyns?" asked Jason, knowing this had been weighing heavily on the colonel's mind. It had been on everyone's minds.

"Not yet. I thought I would wait another day or two and see what other information we might be able to find. The people down on Earth will not be happy with that report."

"What do you think they will do?" asked Jason, looking at the silent bodies on the tables and wondering what this ship had been like when it was fully operational. Now its crew was dead and the ship was wrecked.

Greene looked down at the floor, then over at Jason. "I don't know, but exploring and learning everything about this wreck is going to become a national, if not world wide, priority."

"This Hocklyn threat may be hard for some to accept. Even after hearing it from the computer, it still seems so unreal."

"That's why it's important that we learn as much as we can. This ship alone should be proof enough of what the computer said."

Jason nodded and stood looking at the dead humans. He wondered what type of lives they had lived. Had they actually witnessed the destruction of their worlds? Jason hoped not. He couldn't imagine anything more horrifying than to watch everything you know come to an end and being powerless to stop it.

Greg was exploring with Lisa Gordon down a long corridor with a large hatch at the end of it. Lisa had downloaded some information from the ship's computer and was trying to find the ship's library. The computer had told them there was a room for the crew to enjoy something called holo vids and other entertainment. One of those forms of entertainment mentioned were books.

One of the rules they had implemented now required all exploration of the ship to be done by teams of two for everyone's safety. It had taken them nearly forty minutes to reach this spot deep inside the center section. Greg had left a string of the small LED lights behind them. Looking back down the corridor at the dim lights, it gave him a sense of security knowing they marked the way back.

"Do you really think we will find anything useful in this entertainment room?" he asked as they arrived at the large, closed hatch. This would be the third closed hatch they had come across. The first two had opened easily.

He stopped and eyed the obstruction, hoping it would be easy to open. Almost unconsciously he glanced back down the corridor, shining his light. He had a bad habit of doing that. There was no one there; there never was. Just several of the dim glowing LED lights he had placed on the wall. Then the moment passed, and Greg turned back to Lisa.

"I don't know," confessed Lisa, looking over at Greg. "The computer in the Command Center confuses me. It seems to be severely limited in some of its data. In some subjects, it seems to have a lot of knowledge; in others it doesn't know anything. Sometimes I feel as if I'm talking to two different systems. It doesn't make a lot of sense."

"I'm sure there's an explanation," Greg commented. "This computer is from another world; it may not be like the ones at home."

"Perhaps," Lisa responded, doubtfully. "I just feel as if we're missing something important. The answer is there, I just have to find it."

Greg reached forward and turned the large metal handle on the hatch. Much to his relief, it turned easily. With a push of his hand the hatch swung open, revealing another long corridor. The two stepped inside and began walking. Unseen by either of them, the hatch behind them swung back shut and locked.

The AI had been watching their progress. It had ordered the computer to give them the information about the ship's entertainment center and library. Unfortunately, a power feedback from damaged systems had ordered the hatch to close and lock. The AI knew it was a result of the power it had shifted to this area so it could watch the two. Now the AI had a problem. The hatch could only be opened from one side as the circuits were damaged in the section that the two new humans were in. Someone would have to be sent to rescue them. The AI knew that it had no other choice. It would have to reveal itself to the humans still in the Command Center.

Jason and Adam Simmins were in the Command Center, cataloguing the ship's systems and labeling what each one did. They were getting a general idea of the layout of the operating stations. They had Communications, Navigation, Environmental, Sensors, Propulsion, and Weapons so far identified and labeled. They would ask the computer a question about a console and then label the controls and readouts so as to better understand its function.

Jason was bent over another console, studying it, when Adam spoke to him in a nervous voice. "Commander, I think you need to turn around."

Jason stood up, turned around, and froze at the sight in front of him. The large viewscreen on the front wall of the Command Center had come on, and a beautiful woman in her early twenties was on the screen. The view was from her waist up, and she was dressed in some type of dark blue military uniform.

"What's that?" Adam asked breathlessly. "Where did she come from?"

Jason didn't know what they could have done to make the viewscreen come on all by itself. But the girl on the screen was gorgeous. Her deep dark eyes and shoulder length black hair drew his undivided attention. Jason wondered if the ship's computer had caused it. Was this one of the ship's dead officers?

"I am the ship's AI," the woman on the screen spoke with a simple smile. "I have been watching you since you came aboard the Avenger."

Jason was astonished and could hardly speak. "The Avenger? Is that the name of your ship?" he finally forced out, staring at the screen. He knew from his computer systems studies down on Earth what an AI was supposed to be.

"Yes. The Avenger is a light cruiser formerly in the service of the Federation before all of its worlds were destroyed."

"You're the reason the computer has been answering more of our questions," Jason spoke in sudden understanding. He felt his heart pounding, realizing that now they might get all the rest of the answers they had been seeking. "It wasn't the computer, it was you!"

"Yes."

"What did your crew call you?"

"I'm Ariel," the AI responded, her dark eyes focusing on Jason.

"Why did you choose now to make your presence known?"

"You have two crewmembers that have managed to get themselves locked inside a section of the ship. I am afraid it was my fault for feeding some power into that section so I could observe them. You will need to go and open the hatch manually so they can get out."

"Which two crewmembers?" asked Jason, suspecting it was Greg and Lisa. They had gone to check out the ship's recreation center.

"Greg and Lisa," replied the AI, confirming Jason's fear.

Greg and Lisa had found the recreation room. They were surprised to find it was more like a large recreation center. There were tables, chairs, weight equipment, a large number of viewscreens, and other items. There was a lot of other stuff that they had no idea what it was used for. The center was relatively intact as everything was anchored down securely to the floor. Instead of one room, there were several large rooms.

Lisa was walking around opening all the cabinets on one wall of the first room to see what they contained. Opening the largest one, her eyes grew wide when she saw all the books. There were hundreds of books in the large cabinet.

"You found them!" spoke Greg excitedly, looking over Lisa's spacesuited shoulder.

Lisa took down a few and started turning the pages, which wasn't easy to do with the gloves of her spacesuit. After a few minutes, she chose half a dozen that seemed to have a lot of pictures inside. She would study these when they got back to the Command Center. Perhaps it would give them some insight into the people of the Federation. How they lived, what they did for entertainment, and maybe even what their worlds had been like.

"Let's go," she said, turning to face Greg. "We can come back later and pick up some more. I want to show these to the others."

Greg nodded; he would also like to come back down here later and try to figure out just what some of this equipment was for. This holo vid thing sounded intriguing.

The two turned and left the entertainment center, walking slowly back down the corridor. They came to a stop at the sealed hatch.

"How did that close?" Lisa asked, worriedly. She could have sworn they had left it open.

"I don't know," Greg responded uneasily as he tried to turn the handle. It wouldn't budge.

Greg tried to apply even more force, but to no avail. "This isn't good."

"What do we do now?" asked Lisa, trying not to panic. Jason and Adam knew where they had gone, but it might be hours before they came looking.

Before Greg could answer, the handle turned on its own and the hatch swung open. Jason and Adam stood on the other side.

"I'm glad to see you two," Greg said, relieved but wondering what they were doing here. "The hatch shut by itself, and we were sealed in."

"We know," responded Jason, thankful to see that Greg and Lisa were okay.

"How could you know that?" Lisa asked confused. Radios didn't work inside the ship because of all the metal.

"I'll show you," Jason responded with a mysterious smile. "You're not going to believe what just happened in the Command

Center. I can't explain; you have to see it for yourself. Lisa, you're absolutely going to love this."

Everyone was in the Command Center staring at the large viewscreen. Jason had gone by their makeshift quarters and told everyone they needed to come to the Command Center.

"What is it?" asked Colonel Greene, gazing at the young woman on the viewscreen. "Was this a member of the crew? How did you manage to get this image to come up on the screen?"

"Not quite, Colonel Greene," replied Ariel, smiling.

Colonel Greene stepped back, his eyes refocusing sharply on the screen. He had a confused look upon his face. "Okay, what just happened?"

"This is Ariel, the ship's AI," Jason answered with a grin.

"An AI?" gasped Lisa, walking toward the screen to take a closer look. There was excitement showing in her eyes. "Just how sentient is she?"

"Very," Ariel replied with a slight nod of her head. "I have been observing you from the time Commander Strong and Greg first came into the Command Center after their crash landing. I was planning to reveal my presence to you shortly, but a crisis occurred which put two of your crewmembers in jeopardy."

"So that's how you knew we couldn't get back out of that section," spoke Greg, gazing curiously at the screen. This explained the mysterious presence he had felt. It was the AI that had been watching them.

"It was my fault the door shut," confessed Ariel, nodding at Greg. "I was watching you and the power I was using caused the hatch to shut. I appeared in front of Commander Strong and told him what had happened."

"Ariel, what happened to this ship and how long has it been here?" asked Colonel Greene, realizing here was the opportunity finally to learn some valuable information. He didn't want to waste it.

"This is a light cruiser class ship from the Human Federation of Worlds fleet. It was part of an evacuation fleet that reached this solar system in your year 1917."

"An evacuation fleet," Colonel Greene repeated, his head creasing in a frown. If this ship was part of an evacuation fleet, where were the other ships?

"There was a secret base in our home system that the Hocklyns missed," replied Ariel, accessing her memory. "After the Hocklyns succeeded in wiping out our fleet and destroying all the human worlds, the only survivors left in our home system were at this hidden base. Once the Hocklyns left the home system, the survivors escaped in the ships still at the base with the aid of First Fleet."

"How many ships and how many people came here?" Greene asked.

"There were eighteen civilian ships in the evacuation fleet carrying nearly forty thousand survivors." A look of sadness came over the AI.

"Forty thousand," Colonel Greene repeated slowly. "Those must have been some big ships."

"They were. Several of them were colony ships. We landed survey parties on your world to find a place to settle. Before the survey was completed, a number of our people began falling ill. Soon the illness spread throughout the entire civilian population of the fleet. It was a disease that we had never encountered before. Our medical experts were helpless to stop its spread, and then our people started dying. Only the military ships remained unaffected. Their crews hadn't been involved with the surveys and hadn't intermingled with anyone from the civilian ships."

"The Spanish Flu," Greg spoke with sudden realization, recalling his history. Now he knew what the men and women in the medical wards had died from. "The Spanish Flu spread across the world from 1918 to 1920. It reportedly caused as many as fifty million deaths."

"Yes, it was the flu," confirmed Ariel, nodding her head slightly in acknowledgment. "We had no immunity against it. The civilians began dying by the hundreds. Our medical personnel were desperate to find a cure and worked night and day to find one. It was decided to leave your world and go elsewhere. It was obvious there were diseases on your world that the humans of the Federation had no immunity to."

"How did your ship end up on the Moon?" Jason asked. He wanted to know why the Avenger had crashed.

"The flu broke out on the Avenger, striking down most of the crew within 24 hours. It's not known how the flu managed to get on board. The commander thought that a supply shuttle might have carried it over just prior to the flu outbreak."

"So the flu was spreading through your crew. What caused the Avenger to crash on the Moon?" Colonel Greene asked. From a medical standpoint, he could well understand how a population with no immunity to the flu could rapidly fall victim to the deadly disease.

"One of the engineers became delusional and set off an explosive device in main engineering next to our FTL drive. The explosion knocked out our propulsion systems and most of our power sources. We were already in orbit around your moon at the time. The orbit began to decay, and the Avenger crashed into this crater before we could get any of the secondary propulsion systems back on line. Most of the crew died in the crash. The few that survived, including Commander Standel, moved the bodies to the medical center. The center section was relatively intact. It's heavily reinforced since it contains the crew's living quarters, the medical center, and the recreation center."

"Could none of your ships send down rescue craft?" Colonel Greene asked. He couldn't imagine leaving the survivors here to die.

"The survivors on board all had the flu and passed away within 48 hours. The Battle Cruiser StarStrike stayed in orbit and was in constant communication with the commander until he died."

Everyone was quiet for a moment. It was so sad to know that the desperate survivors of a defeated human civilization had come all this way to escape destruction, only to be struck down by a deadly disease.

"Now what?" Lisa asked. She had hundreds of questions she wanted to ask the AI.

"We get the power back up," Ariel responded with a determined smile. "I have had nearly 100 years to figure out what to do."

"Power?" Jason replied with a startled look. "What do you mean power, and what do you hope to accomplish with it?"

"The center section is still airtight, as well as other sections around the Command Center," Ariel replied, her gaze switching to Jason. "This ship has a number of auxiliary vessels. There are two Raven class shuttles in the ship's flight bay. If we jumpstart the main power source on one of them, we can use it to power up a small section of the ship."

"How do we do that?" Adam Simmins asked.

"Auxiliary ships," Greg spoke, his eyes growing wide. "Are these ships still flyable?"

"Possibly," replied Ariel, shifting her gaze over to Greg. "I would have to run a diagnostic check on their key systems. They have been in a vacuum for the past 100 years. The shuttles are extremely durable ships."

Early the next morning, Jason, Greg, and Adam were deep into the damaged section of the ship. Ariel had given them directions how to reach the ship's flight bay. She thought the flight bay was still intact. The bay was located on the bottom of the ship, and Ariel didn't believe the explosion that had taken out the ship's drive systems had reached the flight bay. At least she hoped that it hadn't.

Ariel's sensors in that area were damaged, and she couldn't access the bay to check on its current condition. That was one of the things she wanted Adam to repair. She thought one of the sensor couplings was damaged and needed to be replaced. Adam was carrying a spare, which he was going to install.

"I hope we can get back out of here," Greg commented as he helped Jason and Adam move some wreckage that was blocking their path.

The corridor they were in had obviously been damaged by either the explosion or the crash landing. In several areas, the walls of the corridor were buckled in as if hit by a huge fist. Several small metal ceiling panels, as well as support beams, had fallen across the corridor blocking their path and had to be moved to the side so they could continue.

This section of the ship, while still intact, was dangerous to pass through. Ariel felt this was the only reasonably safe passage to the flight bay. The AI had promised that if they could power up one of the large shuttles and access its power system, then Ariel could power up the emergency environmental systems. She would then be able to make a small section of the undamaged part of the ship habitable.

Jason stopped and put his hands on his spacesuited waist as he gazed down the corridor. "It shouldn't be much farther. We need to go through that hatch up ahead and then down two more levels. There should be a double airlock that leads to the flight bay."

"I hope the flight bay is still intact," Greg said, his tone showing concern. "As much wreckage as we found in this corridor, I can just imagine what the flight bay might be like."

"The more I see of this ship, the more amazed I am," commented Adam, looking into a room that seemed to be full of a lot of damaged electronic equipment. "The technology to build a ship like this is far more advanced than anything we have ever imagined possible."

"Some of their science and technology is incredible," replied Jason in agreement, stepping up next to Adam and gazing into the room. There were shattered viewscreens and heavily damaged control consoles everywhere.

"I wonder if this room had anything to do with their weapon systems?" Greg asked, intrigued. Just from looking, this room was obviously an important control room of some kind. He was still fascinated about what type of weapons these people had used. So far, Ariel had not revealed any of that information.

"Hard to tell," replied Jason, looking over at Greg. "I'm sure the control systems are somewhere. Give us time, Greg; we'll find them."

Jason could just imagine the men and women who must have worked in this room. Thinking of them made Jason think about his own family down on Earth. If his sister could see him now, she would become unglued. If his overly protective sibling knew that he was deep inside a wrecked spacecraft on the surface of the Moon, she would totally freak out. Fortunately, this was something she would probably never know. Jason suspected that the government would be slapping an extremely high security clearance on any information about the wrecked human spaceship.

"Let's go on down the corridor," ordered Jason, ready to move on. "I can see the next hatch up ahead."

"At least Lisa has an easy and exciting job now," Adam said as he turned to follow Jason. "I didn't think we were ever going to pry her away from the AI last night. Colonel Greene had to order her to go get some rest."

"Can't say that I blame her," Jason replied with a smile. "Ariel is a computer scientist's dream come true."

"I noticed that Colonel Greene and Lisa were having a long conversation this morning before we left," Greg commented. "I wonder what that was about?"

"The AI," Jason replied. "Colonel Greene and I made a list last night of what we wanted Lisa to talk to the AI about. We would like more information about the Human Federation of Worlds, as well as these Hocklyns that defeated them."

"Do you think we're going to have to fight these Hocklyns someday?" Greg asked, his eyes turning to look at Jason.

He knew it would be in the future. Someday his great great grandchildren and their generation might be all that would stand between a free humanity and abject slavery. He didn't want to think about the horror that might wait in the not so distant future.

"Probably," replied Jason, taking a deep breath. "I'm afraid we may not have any choice. From what Ariel has told us the Hocklyns are coming, and we have 268 years to prepare. We can only hope that's time enough."

"If the Federation couldn't stop them with their technology, what chance will we have?" asked Greg, wondering if fighting the Hocklyns was a hopeless task.

"We will have time to prepare," Jason replied carefully. "From Ariel, we know what's coming. Perhaps this time it will be different."

They had made it to the hatch. Reaching forward, Jason grasped the handle and was relieved when it turned easily. Pushing against it with his hand it swung open, revealing a flight of stairs that led downward.

"This ship and its technology could make a big difference," Adam said as they stepped through the hatch and started down the stairs. "If we can reverse engineer all of its systems, we can begin building our own fleet someday."

"The AI should help there," added Greg, thinking about all the knowledge the AI might hold the key to. "It may have everything we need to build ships of this type or even more in its memory."

He wondered if his son would fly one of those new wondrous spaceships that lay in the future. He hoped he would follow in his footsteps someday. Perhaps his son would even command a ship like this one.

When they reached the next level, Jason found another hatch blocking their way. This hatch opened easily also and, after stepping through, they walked down the next flight of stairs and entered a short corridor. Jason stopped and looked at what was in front of them. On his left side was a heavily armored hatch. Stepping forward he tried to open it, but the handle refused to budge.

"I don't think we're getting that one open," Greg commented. "It looks as if it's really stuck."

"I think it's the backup control room for the flight bay," spoke Adam, recalling what the AI had said when she was giving them directions. "It's probably locked down. We can't open it until we have some power restored."

Jason nodded and turned around to the other side of the corridor. There was another hatch, and he stepped forward and turned the handle. It opened easily. It was the airlock!

"The flight bay should be through here," he said, stepping inside.

A few moments later, the three exited the airlock and entered the flight bay. They had brought several large, portable lights, which Greg and Adam were carrying. Switching the lights on, they gazed in awe around them.

There were half a dozen spacecraft in the bay. The two large Raven class shuttles were in the center and seemed to be undamaged. However, two of the smaller ships had suffered catastrophic damage. They seemed to be some type of fighter craft. Both had been tossed against the side of the flight bay, either during the explosion or during the crash landing. The two fighter craft were now nothing but mangled pieces of wreckage.

"Don't guess we will be flying those," commented Greg with disappointment in his voice. He took several steps toward the two wrecked fighters to get a better look.

He wondered what type of weapons had been on the space fighters. Some type of lasers or blasters, he thought. He really wanted to talk to the AI about the weapons the ship was equipped with. His curiosity about that was burning inside of him. These two fighter craft were something else he would now have to ask about.

There were two smaller spacecraft on the other side of the big shuttles, and both of these seemed relatively intact. They were box shaped, with small stubby wings on the sides. Probably some type of small supply shuttle used between ships or to the surface.

What held Jason's gaze were the two large shuttles. Each was about forty feet long and fifteen feet wide at their widest point. Both shuttles had short wings for atmospheric use. The nose was tapered and some type of rocket engines were in the back. Jason knew, from his brief talk with Ariel about these shuttles, that they didn't utilize any type of fuel similar to what Earth was currently using.

Greg walked excitedly over to the nearest shuttle. Shining his light across it, he noticed several hard points underneath the wings for missiles.

"This thing is equipped for missiles!" Greg spoke with excitement in his voice. He then turned and walked over to the tapered nose and, examining it, noticed two indentations. Running his gloved hand over the indentations, he wondered what they concealed. "There are two small hatch covers here on the nose. I wonder if they're for some type of energy weapon?"

"Hard to tell," Jason replied as he and Adam walked over to stand next to Greg. "Perhaps we will know more after we talk to Ariel again."

Greg shined his light up higher, and they could see windows in what was clearly the cockpit for the shuttle. The windows were dark and undoubtedly made of some type of strong glass. Greg realized it might not be glass at all, just some clear material that the other humans had used for their cockpit windows.

"Ariel said we can access the shuttle from the hatch on the other side," Adam commented as he gazed in awe at the shuttle. "She said it should be easy to open."

"I hope so," responded Jason, turning to look at Adam. "If we can't get into the shuttle, Ariel's plan for getting more power won't work."

"We'll get in! Do you realize that this ship has more capabilities than anything Earth has ever launched?" Adam said, animatedly. "According to Ariel, this shuttle is equipped with a sublight drive as well as limited FTL capability. If we could get this shuttle back down to Earth and build more like her, we could be exploring the entire Solar System in just a matter of a few years."

"That would be something," commented Gregg, trying to imagine what it would be like to fly to Mars or the other planets in just a matter of a few hours. It was hard to comprehend. He would like to be on one of the flights to Mars. The red planet had always intrigued him.

The three walked around the shuttle and found the entrance hatch. Jason reached forward and touched a small control panel. He punched in a short string of numbers and waited expectantly. Ariel had given them the command codes necessary to enter the shuttle. The hatch slid open, and the three stepped cautiously inside. They found themselves in a small room that was obviously used for passengers. A dozen comfortable seats were against the walls. In the rear, another closed hatch obviously led to the engine compartment, and an open hatch in the front led to the cockpit.

Jason stepped through the front hatch and found himself in a small but efficient cockpit. There were four seats. There were two for the pilot and copilot, and two more seats on the sides in front of other consoles for two other crewmembers. The small cockpit was full of controls and instruments. It reminded him of other cockpits he had been in.

Jason wondered what it would feel like to fly something like this. He could recall the exhilarating thrills back in his test pilot days when he had flown experimental jets. The first few times flying this shuttle would be very similar.

Adam stepped around Jason and looked at a printout he was carrying. He moved over and checked a control panel next to one of the side consoles. Several screens on the panel were glowing dimly. "Battery power is at twelve percent; not enough to jump start the shuttle's main power source. We were expecting that."

"So we need to lug the other RTG power source down here and hook it up to this shuttle," commented Greg, grimacing at the thought of dragging the unit down all those corridors and stairs.

"It won't be that hard," replied Jason, knowing what Greg was thinking. "It will just be tedious and something that has to be done." Turning to Adam, he asked. "Do you see any problems with hooking our power source up to the shuttle?"

"No," answered Adam, standing up from where he had been bending over the console. "With the information that Ariel has given us, it should be quite simple."

"Let's go back and get the RTG then," Jason said. "The sooner we get the power up in this shuttle, the sooner we will have easier access to the rest of the ship."

"I want to install the sensor relay before we leave," Adam stated. "That will allow Ariel to monitor what we're doing, and she can talk us through any problems we might run into."

"Very well," replied Jason, nodding his head in agreement. "Let's get the relay installed and then we can go get the RTG."

Chapter Four

Two days later, everyone waited expectantly to see what would happen when power was restored to the undamaged sections of the ship. Greg and Adam were down in the flight bay, and the rest were in the Command Center.

"Should be anytime now," spoke Marcus, glancing down at his watch.

Without warning, the panels in the Command Center all lit up, and the overhead lights panels came on brilliantly. They all jumped when one of the panels exploded in a shower of sparks.

"Don't panic," Ariel spoke quickly. "It was just a power surge."

She was busily adjusting the power coming from the shuttle, rapidly shutting down areas of the ship that were damaged or where power wasn't needed. There were numerous areas where power leads were broken or completely nonexistent. It took her several minutes to seal off all the areas where she didn't want power going. The only areas that needed power were the flight bay, the area around the Command Center, and the central section. Once she was satisfied everything was working properly, she issued some specific commands to the computer to allow it to monitor the power.

"What's happening, Ariel?" Lisa asked concerned. Her eyes were frantically looking around the command center for any other problems. The exploding overhead light had shaken her up considerably.

"I'm scanning the ship to see what other resources may be available for power. The primary and secondary high-energy fusion reactors were destroyed or damaged in the initial explosion that took out the sublight and FTL systems. The resulting crash caused further damage."

"Are there other power sources on the ship?" Colonel Greene asked. This was something Ariel hadn't mentioned before.

"There is a small emergency reactor for the weapon systems which I am trying to access to determine its usability."

"Is it safe to turn on after all these years?" Colonel Greene asked, nervously. He didn't want to see the wrecked ship blow up in a massive explosion. If the human race was to have a chance against the Hocklyns, they had to preserve what was left of the Avenger.

"Quite safe," Ariel replied with a gentle smile. "There are sufficient fail safes and redundancies built into the Avenger's systems to prevent a core breach or a failure of any of the reactor's primary systems."

"That's a relief," spoke Greg, shaking his head. "I didn't really want to glow in the dark."

Ariel was quiet for a moment, and then a pleased smile appeared on her young face. "Reactor has been activated, and power is coming online. Standby for reactivation of artificial gravity field."

"What?" Jason stammered as he suddenly felt his weight increase until it was normal. "How the hell did you do that?"

Ariel looked embarrassed as she gazed at Jason. "Oh, did I forget to mention that all Federation ships had an artificial gravity field? The field is also used to counter excessive acceleration and deceleration. The ship can maneuver at speeds of up to twelve gravities with no harmful effects to the crew. Or at least the Avenger used to be able to do that before it crashed."

Two hours later, all six explorers were down in the center section. Power had been restored, and the environmental control systems were working. Ariel had directed them to a section where the ship's officers had stayed. The quarters in this area were roomy and extremely comfortable.

"A real bed," Greg spoke with a wide grin, looking into one of the spacious rooms. Some cleaning and organizing and the quarters would be livable.

"We need more people up here," spoke Colonel Greene, glancing into the quarters he had chosen. "Ariel says the ship's oxygen is recyclable and should last for several more years, even with a larger group of people on board."

Lisa came out of the quarters she had chosen with a big smile on her face. "We actually have running water and toilets!"

"What about the bodies in the medical center?" Greg asked with concern.

"Ariel is keeping the temperature in those rooms at a low enough temperature to preserve them," Colonel Greene responded. "That won't be a problem."

"What's next?" Adam asked.

Having the environmental systems back up and running would allow them to check out more of the ship's systems and the science behind them. Working in the cumbersome spacesuits was a pain. Now, in many areas, they might not have to.

"I want us all to meet in a couple of hours after we get our quarters organized," Greene spoke with a thoughtful look on his face. "We need to go over everything we have learned so far and figure out our next steps. Having the power on is going to make a big difference in our explorations of this ship."

"We have learned a lot the last few days," added Jason, nodding his head in agreement. "This ship and Ariel have a lot to teach us."

"We have to learn and learn quickly," continued Colonel Greene, agreeing with Jason. "Every moment lost is one moment closer to the Hocklyns finding us. We must begin preparing for that day as soon as possible. The future of the human race may rest with what we learn from this ship."

-

All six of the explorers were sitting in a small conference room next to the Command Center. Jason wondered what kind of meetings might have been held in this room in years past. He could imagine the commander standing at the front of the table and explaining to his officers the latest developments in the war. Jason could scarcely imagine how it had affected them when their worlds had been destroyed and they found themselves powerless to stop it.

"Okay, let's get this meeting started," spoke Colonel Greene, setting down a pile of reports and photographs on the table in front of him. "Lisa, if you will begin, please tell us what you have found out about the AI and the worlds this ship came from."

Lisa nodded and brushed a strand of wayward blonde hair out of her eyes. "First, let's start with the AI. Ariel is not a true AI."

"What?" Greg stammered in confusion. "She sure seems real enough to me."

"She is a highly sophisticated computer with some very advanced programming," Lisa explained. "This programming allows her to act and to respond as if she is a real person. The programming I have examined so far allows her a limited amount of freedom to make some decisions on her own. Even so, these programs do control her actions, and she can't violate them."

"Interesting," commented Colonel Greene, leaning back in his chair. "What about the human worlds this ship came from?"

"I did manage to get that information from Ariel," continued Lisa, nodding her head. She turned her deep blue eyes toward the colonel. "The Human Federation of Worlds comprised five inhabited solar systems and a number of scientific and mining outposts in approximately twenty others."

"Sounds impressive," spoke Jason, wondering how long it would take for Earth to grow that large. He leaned forward. "Do you know what their population was?"

"From the information I have gathered, it was slightly over fourteen billion at the time of the first Hocklyn attack."

"Fourteen billion," mumbled Adam, shaking his head sadly. "So many people."

"All wiped out by the Hocklyns," Colonel Greene reminded everyone. "And those same Hocklyns are coming for us in another 268 years."

"Do we have any idea what the Hocklyns look like?" Greg asked, curiously. Surely, the humans on this ship had known what their enemy looked like.

"Yes, we do," replied Colonel Greene, reaching forward and retrieving several photographs. He passed these around the table.

Greg took one and his eyes widened at what he was seeing. The Hocklyns looked like a lizard that walked on two feet with arms and hands. They were a pale green in color with a small crest on the top of their head. Looking closer, he noticed that the fingers on the hands were unusually long and double-jointed. Not only that, instead of five digits, there were six.

"The Hocklyns obviously come from a reptilian ancestry," Colonel Greene spoke his eyes looking around the small group. "Their skin is reported to be covered with very fine scales, and their body temperature is below what humans would call normal. Their blood chemistry is also markedly different. The Hocklyns are a very harsh and cruel race. They live to improve and grow their empire. Nothing else matters."

"And they are coming for us sometime in the future," Greg said, still gazing at the picture. These aliens could never be allowed to conquer Earth!

"Yes, they are," responded Colonel Greene. "They are an unstoppable force, and we are in their path."

The meeting lasted for nearly an hour, with each member of the team reporting on the progress of his or her studies and the exploration of the ship. They now had a pretty good feel for the layout of the Avenger. Toward the end of the meeting, Colonel Greene had some assignments for the explorers.

"Tomorrow Jason, Greg, and Adam will be going to the Environmental section," spoke Greene, looking at the assignments for the following day. "We want to see how well the systems are working and whether it is feasible to bring more people up here. There are two corridors which are still airtight and should allow you easy access."

"What has Earth said about all of this?" Jason asked, curiously. He could well imagine the impact their discoveries were having on the politicians.

"I have sent Mission Control complete reports of everything we have discovered so far," Greene replied in a serious tone. "Tom Hays told me that the President was calling an emergency meeting with several other heads of state to discuss the situation."

"The fire's about to start burning," commented Greg, meeting the colonel's eyes.

He had talked briefly to his wife that morning, and she had inquired about what was going on. She had said there were all sorts of rumors flying around. Particularly since it had been revealed that a second lander had been sent to the Moon. Greg had tried to reassure her that everything was fine. But he could sense the doubt and worry in her voice. He really needed to get home to his family.

Jason was standing in the Command Center, shaking his head. He could scarcely believe what he had just heard. "I don't understand. Are you saying that both of the shuttles are still flyable?"

"That's correct," replied Ariel, nodding her head. "I have run a full diagnostic check on both of them and they are flyable."

"How safe are they to fly?" asked Colonel Greene, sitting down at a console and staring at the front viewscreen. "What would be the risk in sending one of the shuttles back to Earth to pick up more personnel and to return here?"

"Minimal," Ariel replied, confidently. "Even in the shuttles there are enough redundant systems to ensure a safe trip."

Colonel Greene was quiet for a moment as he weighed his options. Then he turned to face Jason. "If I were to send you and Greg back to Earth immediately, how would you feel about that?"

Jason hesitated for a moment. "I know Greg really wants to get home to his family. My own family has been asking a lot of questions. I would like to go back too, but I would like the option of returning to help study this ship at a later date. There is so much to learn here, and I want to be part of it."

"I think that can be arranged," replied Greene, nodding his head as he reached a decision. "The people on the ground need to hear firsthand what we have learned up here. You can only put so much in a report."

"How soon do we leave?" asked Jason, suddenly realizing they were going home.

He knew his brother and sister would be thrilled to see him. He hadn't realized until this moment just how much he had missed them. The thought of going home had brought those feelings to the surface.

"As soon as it can be arranged," replied Greene, leaning back and watching Jason. "We have to figure out a safe place to land and hide the shuttle. It may be necessary to keep your return a secret for a few months. It would be hard to explain how the two of you managed to suddenly reappear down on Earth."

"What about our families?" Jason asked. It would be terrible to return home and still not be able to see their families.

"I think something can be arranged," Greene said, confidently. "According to Ariel, we can have the other shuttle fully prepped and ready to fly the day after tomorrow. We will also have to make some special arrangements with Mission Control. We're sending them a spacecraft that's at least a hundred years more advanced than anything they have ever flown."

"We're going to open some eyes down on Earth," said Jason, smiling. He could just imagine the impression the shuttle would make with the engineers and technicians down on Earth. "This shuttle will make them realize just what it is we have discovered here on the Moon."

"It will also help to emphasize the danger our world is in," Greene replied, determinedly. "We have to make them understand the seriousness of the danger the Hocklyns represent. Just seeing this shuttle and realizing that the people that built it were soundly defeated should make them realize just what the future generations of our world will be up against. Now, why don't you go tell Greg he's going home."

"That's one thing I definitely will enjoy doing," replied Jason, smiling. He knew that Greg would be thrilled at the news.

Two days later, Jason and Greg were in the second shuttle. Jason was in the pilot's seat, and Greg was sitting next to him in the copilot's seat.

"This is sure strange," spoke Greg, looking out the large cockpit window toward the hangar doors, which were still shut. "I never expected to be returning to Earth in something like this."

"Just imagine the impact our landing will make," replied Jason with a grin.

"White Sands, New Mexico," responded Greg, shaking his head. "That's a long ways from where we took off."

"But it's secure and controlled by the military," continued Jason, recalling all the discussion about finding a secure and safe landing site. "They have a special hangar ready for us. We're landing at night, and the sky is overcast above White Sands. Hopefully no one will spot us."

"They wouldn't be able to anyway," Ariel spoke over the com system. "The shuttle's stealth systems will be activated as soon as you leave the Moon."

"Are you sure this is safe?" Greg asked Ariel for the tenth time since he had found out they were returning to Earth. Tom Hays had assured him that his wife would be waiting when they landed at White Sands. He didn't want to crash.

"Perfectly safe, Greg," Ariel replied evenly. "This type of shuttle has an extremely good safety record."

"Yeah, but this one has been setting around unused for nearly 100 years," Greg added, worriedly.

"Launch in five minutes, Commander Strong," Ariel reported. "Flight bay is being depressurized."

Jason looked out the cockpit window at the large hangar doors. The next hurdle would be to get the doors open. Ariel was pretty confident they would open, but they hadn't been tested.

"Opening hangar doors," Ariel reported.

One of the doors slid open easily; the second didn't budge.

"One of the doors didn't open," Jason informed Ariel over the radio. She had explained to him how to operate the shuttle's communication equipment.

"I'm working on it," Ariel replied. "The door seems to be bent. I don't think it's going to open."

"Crap," Greg replied disappointed. He felt sick at his stomach knowing they might not be able to launch the shuttle. He had really been looking forward to seeing his wife and baby.

"No problem," Ariel responded after a moment. "We can launch the shuttle through the open door. There will be two feet of clearance on both sides."

"Two feet!" moaned Greg turning pale. "Is that safe?"

"Perfectly safe," Ariel replied as she sent the commands to the shuttle to begin powering up its sublight engine.

Jason felt the shuttle rise above the deck in the flight bay. It hovered for a moment, then slowly moved toward the open door. He felt tense, and he could feel his heart beating faster. The shuttle approached the open door and then passed through it. Looking out the cockpit window, he saw the shuttle's wing barely clear the door. Once outside, the shuttle tilted upward and began to accelerate rapidly. In moments, they were in space above the Moon.

"This is amazing," spoke Greg in awe, gazing out the cockpit window on his side as the Moon began to drop rapidly away.

"Two hours to Earth," responded Jason, recalling the flight plan. "Who would have ever thought something like this could be possible?"

He leaned back in his seat, trying to relax. His sister and brother would be waiting for him at White Sands. They were still discussing at Mission Control just what Greg and he could tell their families about what had happened on the Moon. They would have to be told something, how else could they explain their sudden appearance down on Earth?

The shuttle continued toward Earth, its stealth fields having been activated as the shuttle left the Moon. As it approached Earth's atmosphere the shuttle began to slow, then entered a gentle arc toward its destination.

Jason looked down at the Earth below. It was dark over the United States, but the country was lit up by all the city lights. This was his home, and he was glad to be returning. There was a time a few weeks back when he had wondered if he would ever see this sight again.

"It's beautiful," Greg spoke, wistfully. "I wish Elizabeth could see this."

"Perhaps someday she might," responded Jason, looking over at his close friend. "With the technology we're going to learn from Ariel and from the Avenger, space travel might become extremely common in a few more years."

The shuttle continued its descent. A few minutes later, the landing lights at White Sands came into view. The shuttle followed them and then entered a large, brightly lit hangar. As soon as the shuttle was inside, it gently landed and the hangar doors slid shut.

"We're here," said Greg, standing up. He hoped his wife and son were waiting. He could hardly wait to see them.

"Let's go out and see what type of welcoming party we have," Jason replied. It felt good to be back on Earth.

Moments later, they stepped out of the shuttle to be greeted by a large crowd of military people and technicians. Tom Hays was the first one to greet them.

"Welcome back," he said enthusiastically, pumping their hands, and then looked over at the shuttle. "This is great! It's a new day for our world, all thanks to the two of you!"

Jason nodded. It might be great for today, but the Hocklyns waited in the future.

Tom led the two outside the hangar where a vehicle was waiting. Minutes later, they found themselves inside an office. Jason looked over at Greg, suspecting that their debriefing was about to begin. The door opened and, much to his surprise, his sister and brother stepped through. Right behind them was Greg's wife, carrying their infant son.

"Elizabeth!" yelled Greg, jumping up. He rushed over and kissed his wife, then gave both his wife and son an affectionate hug.

"Oh, Greg," responded Elizabeth, starting to cry.

Jason walked over to his sister and brother. Trevor reached out and shook Jason's hand. "I'm glad you're back, big brother. I don't understand how, but I'm glad."

Katherine stepped forward and hugged Jason. "I don't know how you can always get into so much trouble. I warned you about going to the Moon. What happened?"

Jason took a deep breath. How could he explain all of this? Tom Hays had told them not to talk to anyone yet about what had happened on the Moon. There would be a briefing in the morning in which Greg and he would be told what they could reveal. "You won't believe it," he responded with a big smile. "I will tell you about it in the morning. Now I just want to hear what you and Trevor have been doing while I've been gone."

Greg was holding his infant son. Deep in his heart he knew that someday his son would be flying a new generation of spaceships. They would soon be building spaceships capable of traveling to the stars. His son would see things that Greg could only imagine. But for now he was happy. He took his wife's hand and looked down at his son. Life couldn't be any better.

Back on the Moon, Colonel Greene and Lisa were talking to Ariel. There was a question Colonel Greene had been meaning to ask the AI.

"Ariel, do you know what solar system your people went to after they left ours back in 1917?"

Ariel looked back at Colonel Greene in surprise. "I never said they left this solar system. They are still here."

"What!" Colonel Greene exploded, his face turning pale. "What do you mean they're still here?"

"My people came here to seek refuge on Earth as well as to build a new military base. When it became obvious that due to the diseases down on Earth they couldn't live there, they went on to build the new base."

"Where is this base?" Colonel Greene asked, slowly. He looked over at Lisa. Her eyes were wide in disbelief.

"It's inside the asteroid Ceres," replied Ariel, looking at Colonel Greene, confused. "I told you at the very beginning that they were going to establish a base in this solar system."

"Have you heard from them since the crash?"

"No," Ariel replied.

"This is going to be big news back on Earth," commented Colonel Greene, shaking his head in disbelief. How was he going to explain this to the people in Mission Control? Tom Hays was going to be stunned at this news.

"Ariel, can one of the shuttles make it to Ceres and back safely?"

"Yes, Colonel; it shouldn't be a problem. I have been curious myself as to why there has been no contact with the base since the survivors went there."

"I think we have a new mission for Commander Strong. As soon as he has taken a few weeks off, I think he will be flying to Ceres."

Back on Earth, Jason and Greg were going out to eat with their families. Tom Hays had told them that a special meal had been prepared to celebrate their return in the cafeteria. Little did Jason suspect what was waiting in his future. If he thought the Moon had held a surprise it wouldn't compare to what was waiting inside the asteroid Ceres.

The End

Moon Wreck: Secrets of Ceres

Chapter One

Jason Strong was relaxing on the front porch of his home, watching the sunset. His house was located in a quiet suburb away from most of the noises and crowds that plagued the city. It had been six weeks since Greg and he had returned from their perilous Moon mission. The clouds above the horizon glowed red and orange-red in the fading light. The colors were a stark contrast to the blacks and grays of the lunar surface that he had become so familiar with.

Even now, he still had occasional nightmares about the lunar lander and the crash landing. Letting out a deep breath, he watched curiously as a car pulled into the driveway. His eyes narrowed, now who could that be, he wondered. He wasn't expecting anyone and very few people even knew that he was home. He heard the front door open and sensed that his sister Katherine had stepped out onto the porch. Glancing at her, he saw that she was watching the car as if a dangerous predator had just arrived. She had been overly protective since he had returned from his Moon mission.

The car door opened, and Tom Hays climbed out. Tom was the director of Mission Control in Houston. He waved at Jason, and then turned to say something to someone else in the car. The passenger door opened, and a man dressed in a military uniform appeared. Jason stood up, frowning. What was Tom Hays doing here with a military general?

"Jason, whatever they want, tell them no," Katherine spoke in a low and concerned voice. "You've already done enough."

The two men walked up to the porch and climbed the steps.

"Hello Jason," Tom Hays spoke in a pleasant voice. "This is General Adamson from the Pentagon."

Jason shook the hands of both men. "We finished my final debriefing two weeks ago," Jason said, wondering what the men wanted. "I believe we covered everything that occurred on the Moon."

"This isn't about your debriefing," General Adamson replied in a firm military voice. "Is there somewhere we can go and talk privately?"

"I have a small office in the house," answered Jason, looking over at his sister. He could tell from the dark look in her eyes that she wasn't happy with these visitors.

"Remember what I said?" Katherine spoke, her eyes turning dark. "You've already put yourself in enough danger."

"Jason's done a great service for this country," spoke Tom looking at Katherine. "What he accomplished on the Moon was a miracle."

Tom understood Katherine's anxiety. He could still remember her living at Mission Control when they had lost contact with the New Beginnings mission. She had waited with a haunted look in her eyes for any word from her brother. She had been there almost the entire time until Jason and Greg managed to shut down the emergency beacon on the crashed spaceship and reestablished radio contact with Mission Control.

"Just remember that," replied Katherine, looking directly at Tom. "He doesn't need to do any more!"

"Relax, Katherine," Jason said with a reassuring smile. "We're just going to talk."

"That better be all," replied Katherine, giving Jason a warning glance.

Jason led the two men into the house and through a door that led to his office. He sat down in his favorite chair and gestured for the other two men to take a seat on the comfortable sofa that was against the wall in front of the window. During the day, the window let in just enough light to make Jason's office more inviting. "What can I do for you?" asked Jason, looking over at Tom Hayes. "I'm sure you didn't come all this way just for a social call."

"You're right, Jason. Something's come up," admitted Tom, glancing over at General Adamson. He took a deep breath before continuing. "What I am about to tell you is top secret. Right after Greg and you left the Moon, there was a startling discovery."

"I imagine there will be a lot of startling discoveries in that wreck," Jason replied with a slight smile. "It's not every day you find a wrecked spaceship on the Moon and an AI like Ariel."

"No, it isn't," agreed General Adamson, leaning forward. "You did a fantastic job up there, Commander Strong. But now we have something else we need you to do."

Jason leaned back in his chair and folded his arms across his chest. He had hoped to spend at least a few more weeks with his sister and brother before going back to work. From the look on the faces of Tom and the general, that wasn't going to happen.

"What's going on?" he asked, his eyes narrowing. "What's Colonel Greene discovered now?"

Tom took another deep breath before beginning. "Immediately after you left, Ariel made a shocking statement. It was something that Colonel Greene and Lisa Gordon were not expecting and couldn't believe."

"Ariel has a way of doing that," responded Jason, recalling the gorgeous AI. "She's not human and doesn't think like we do."

The AI on the Avenger had surprised him on several occasions. Particularly the first time she had appeared in the Command Center and told him and Adam Simmons that Greg and Lisa were trapped behind a sealed hatch in the ship.

"You remember that she explained that the survivors from the Human Federation of Worlds came down with the Spanish Flu when they arrived here," spoke Tom, knowing that Jason was familiar with this. They had discussed this during Jason's debriefing.

"Yes. The flu spread through their fleet, killing hundreds. They gave up the idea of setting up a colony on Earth and left. That's why the Avenger crashed. A sick engineer destroyed or damaged their drive systems, disabling the ship as it passed the Moon. The Moon's gravity pulled it down, causing it to crash in the crater."

"The problem was we forgot to ask Ariel where the survivors went when she first mentioned this. Everyone assumed they had gone on to another solar system," General Adamson said with a troubled look in his eyes.

"Of course they did," Jason replied with a confused look. "Where else could they go? There isn't another habitable planet in our Solar System. It only made sense that they find another solar system with a suitable planet they could colonize."

General Adamson shook his head slowly and his eyes narrowed. "We all forgot why they came here. They came here to set up a colony on Earth and to establish a new military base."

"I don't understand," Jason replied, suddenly feeling uneasy. He looked intently at Tom. "The colony on Earth wasn't feasible due to their lack of immunity to Earth diseases. They had to go on to another solar system."

"That's not what happened," replied General Adamson, shaking his head.

"According to Ariel, these humans never left the Solar System. They're still here," Tom spoke in a level voice, gazing into Jason's eyes.

"They're still here!" Jason sputtered, his eyes growing wide in disbelief. "That's not possible. There has been no trace of them on Earth. If they were here, we would know about it. You can't hide ships as big as theirs."

"They're not on Earth," explained General Adamson, shaking his head. He let out a deep breath, and then continued. "According to Ariel, they went on and built their military base here in our Solar System."

"Where?" asked Jason, feeling a chill of excitement run down his back. Was it possible some of these humans were still alive? Was there some way they could be contacted?

"According to Ariel, the military part of their fleet had always planned on building a new and powerful military base in our Solar System as a means of protecting Earth," Adamson continued. "They had planned on leaving most of the civilians down on Earth in the new colony, and then the military ships would go on and construct their new base. The base would be responsible for defending Earth until we were ready to defend ourselves."

Jason could hardly believe what the general was saying. "So you're saying that somewhere in our Solar System is a fully operational military base of the Human Federation of Worlds?"

"That's just it," Tom broke in, shaking his head worriedly. "Ariel has never heard from nor seen any of their ships since the Avenger crashed. The AI had a few short-range scanners still working immediately after the crash. In recent years, as her power supply dropped, she could only scan the area immediately around the Earth and the Moon. There were even times when she was in a standby mode and was awakened periodically by the ship's computer. However, in the 100 years since the ship crashed she has never detected another ship. It's as if the survivors vanished."

"It's a shame we don't know where they went," Jason commented, feeling disappointed. He would give anything to see one of their warships intact. Even the civilian ships would be amazing. An intact ship could mean so much to Earth's future war effort against the Hocklyns.

"We do know," General Adamson said, gazing intently at Jason. "They went to the asteroid Ceres."

"Ceres," spoke Jason, drawing in a sharp breath. For a moment, he was silent, thinking about what the general had just said. He knew that Ceres was the largest asteroid in the Solar System. "Surely if they're on Ceres we could detect or see something. Their ships are too big to stay hidden."

"We've tried searching for signs of artificial structures on Ceres, as well as their ships," Tom replied with a heavy sigh. "We've used telescopes and every detecting device we have. There's nothing! No sign of their ships or any artificial constructions on or around the asteroid."

"Perhaps after the flu struck them, they decided to change their plans and go on to another solar system," Jason suggested. "Not being able to plant a colony on Earth may have left them with no other choice."

"Perhaps," Tom replied, doubtfully. "But I just can't see them leaving Earth undefended. Not with their knowledge of the Hocklyns and what Earth would be facing in the future."

"This all sounds interesting," spoke Jason, leaning forward and placing his hands on his desk. "Ariel never mentioned any of this while I was there. I want to go back up to the Avenger someday to help with the research, but how does this missing fleet involve me?"

General Adamson looked down at the floor and then gazed directly at Jason with an extremely serious look upon his face. "We want you to take one of the Raven shuttles that are on the Avenger and go to Ceres. We want you to find out what happened to the survivors of that fleet after they left Earth."

Jason sat silently, not believing what he had just heard. His head felt as if it was spinning. Then focusing, he thought about what the general had just said. "Why me?"

"You're familiar with the Avenger and the situation up there," Tom began. "You handled the situation up on the Moon extremely well. We need someone like you to lead this mission."

Jason looked at the two and had a feeling they were not telling him everything. "What else is there? There has to be another reason."

Tom looked extremely uncomfortable. He looked over at the general, who nodded.

"It's Ariel," confessed Tom sounding slightly annoyed "She will not allow us to use one of the shuttles unless you command the mission."

"What?" Jason spoke, surprised, his eyes growing wide. "Why is she demanding that?"

"She says she trusts you," Tom replied. "If there are survivors in Ceres, Ariel feels you will do the right thing. I know you wanted some more time off, but this is really important."

"Is she demanding anyone else to go on this mission?" Jason asked with a sudden suspicion.

"Ariel wants Greg also," Tom admitted uncomfortably, looking over at General Adamson. "Lisa Gordon and Adam Simmins are also among those she wants."

"How many others will there be?" asked Jason, trying to think if he actually wanted to do this. Those shuttles were over 100 years old, and Ceres wasn't exactly close to Earth.

"There will be eight on the shuttle," General Adamson responded. "We are still deciding on the other four."

"How safe will this trip be?" asked Jason, thinking about what they were asking him to do. It was one thing to fly those shuttles between the Earth and the Moon. Ceres was millions of miles away!

"Ariel has a group of our technicians going over one of the shuttles, checking all of its systems. It should be ready in two more weeks. She has assured us that the shuttle will have no problems making the trip to Ceres and returning."

Jason let out a sharp breath. He felt excitement growing at just the thought of making this trip. This was a rare opportunity to travel far out into the Solar System. He might never get this chance again. Who knew what they might find on Ceres. "If I agree, when do we leave?"

"We would need you and Greg back up on the Moon by the end of the week," General Adamson replied. "Both of you will have to go through a crash course on how to fly and operate the shuttle. Ariel claims she can operate the shuttle by remote control all the way to Ceres and back, but I would feel better if the crew could pilot and operate it in an emergency."

"Will you do it, Jason?" asked Tom, knowing he was asking a lot. "This mission could be more important than finding the Avenger. There may be intact ships inside Ceres if the base was actually built. Imagine what that could mean."

Jason closed his eyes. He knew his sister was going to be highly upset with him again. She knew they had found a crashed spaceship on the Moon. He had been allowed to tell her and Trevor that, but nothing else. Jason also wondered how Greg would feel about this. He wasn't sure Greg would be willing to leave his wife and infant son so soon after returning from the Moon. It had been extremely difficult for Greg to be away from his family, not knowing if he would ever see them again.

"Well?" General Adamson asked. "We will do everything in our power to make sure you have everything you need to accomplish this mission safely. We need to know what's on Ceres."

Jason slowly nodded his head. There had never been any real doubt in his mind that he was going to accept. The crucial question now was how was he going to explain all of this to Greg? An even bigger problem was how was he going to explain this to his sister?

Greg leaned back in his chair and closed his eyes slowly, shaking his head. He couldn't believe what Jason had just asked him to do. For the last two weeks, he had concentrated on his family, getting to know his infant son and enjoying the feeling of being a father. Now Jason was asking him to give that up and go on a dangerous mission from which he might not return.

"Ceres," he mumbled, trying to recall what he knew about the distant asteroid. "That's a long way to go in a 100 year old shuttle."

"Ariel and some technicians are checking the shuttle," replied Jason, trying to sound positive. "She says we can do this."

"Lisa and Adam will be going too?" asked Greg, wondering what he should do. How could he explain this to his wife? He had very mixed feelings about this mission. Part of him was screaming to go; the other was asking what about Elizabeth?

"Yes, and there will be four others besides them," added Jason, knowing that Greg was struggling with this decision. He couldn't blame him. "General Adamson promised that if anything goes wrong, the second shuttle will be used to launch a rescue mission."

Greg could feel his heart pounding in his chest. He genuinely wanted to go, but was it fair to his family? The ordeal he had put his wife through when Jason and he had crashed on the Moon was still fresh in his mind. They were just now getting where they could talk about it without his wife breaking into tears.

"We have to leave by the end of the week?" asked Greg, his mind racing. That wasn't a lot of time.

"Yes," responded Jason, knowing that was only a few days away. "General Adamson wants us to go through training on how to fly and operate the shuttle. It should take about two weeks."

"Makes sense," Greg replied slowly with a pained look on his face. "Jason, I need to talk to Elizabeth. This is a decision I can't make without speaking to her. After what I put her through when our lander crashed, I just can't do this without her permission."

"I understand," replied Jason, nodding his head. He knew that Greg placed a lot of importance on his family. "I told General Adamson you would have to talk it over with Elizabeth. He has given you permission to tell her about going to Ceres but not much more than that. Greg, if this is going to put a strain on your family you don't have to go. I'm sure Ariel will understand."

"I'll let you know tomorrow," Greg said, letting out a deep breath. He knew he would have to have a long talk with Elizabeth. However, one of his greatest dreams was to get to explore space. He didn't want to miss out on this opportunity. He might never get another.

Jason was sitting in the copilot's seat on board the shuttle Ariel had sent down to retrieve him and Greg. Greg was back in the revamped passenger compartment talking to a new group of technicians and scientists that were going up to the Avenger. The scientists were full of questions after learning who Greg was and that he had spent a number of weeks on the wrecked spaceship. Jason was glad Greg was going. He knew that if Greg had decided not to go, his best friend would have regretted that decision later.

Looking out the cockpit window, Jason saw the Moon rapidly growing in size. He doubted if he would ever get used to traveling at these speeds. A trip that once took days now took only a matter of a few hours. "How many people are currently on the Avenger?" asked Jason, looking over at the young man who was sitting in the pilot's seat.

"There are forty-two, plus the eight we are bringing up on this trip," the young lieutenant replied. "Colonel Greene is really pushing the exploration of the ship. They're also cataloguing and looking extremely close at all the wreckage strung across the crater. Some of it has even been brought into the flight bay to be studied."

Jason nodded, wondering what he would find when they landed. He noticed a slight change in the shuttle's trajectory, and he knew they were now descending toward the desolate lunar surface.

"We did manage to get the other hangar door working," the lieutenant added. He had been told that during the first few launches only one door would open, leaving a clearance of only a few feet on each side of the shuttle's wings.

The Moon's desolate surface rapidly grew nearer and soon the shuttle leveled off, heading toward a small crater in the distance. Reaching the crater, the shuttle slowly circled and for the first time Jason had a good view of the wreck. It was still difficult to see unless you understood just what you were looking at. He knew that the large boulders and clumps of rocks below were actually dust-covered pieces of the Avenger.

Jason hadn't realized until now just how much wreckage was in the crater. It made him wonder exactly how large the Avenger had been before the crash. Looking toward the Avenger, he could see the remains of the crashed ship. It dwarfed everything else in the crater. The wreck was nearly 400 feet long and 200 feet high. Jason's eyes moved along the ship, looking at all of the closed hatches and noticing several that had been opened. The Federation had certainly known how to build ships.

"Colonel Greene is waiting for you and your friend in the conference room next to the Command Center," the lieutenant continued as he watched the instruments on the flight control panel. The ship was being flown by remote control, but he knew enough to take over in case of an emergency.

The shuttle arrowed down slightly, and Jason saw that the two large doors to the flight bay were open. Moments later, the shuttle entered smoothly and sat down gently on the deck. There wasn't even a slight jar as the shuttle came to a complete stop and the engines shut off.

Taking a deep breath, Jason unfastened his flight harness and stood up. He was back where all of this had begun over twelve weeks ago. Going into the passenger compartment, he saw the hatch was already open and the other passengers were exiting.

"Guess we're back," Greg said, smiling broadly. He was excited to find out what had been discovered in their absence. He hoped he would get the opportunity to inspect the Avenger's weapons before they had to leave to go to Ceres.

He was glad that his wife had agreed to let him come. Their talk had been quite long and comprehensive, but she understood his desire to be part of this. She had made him promise to come back safely.

"There are over 50 people up here now," responded Jason, walking over to stand next to Greg. "Colonel Greene has brought a lot of specialists up here to help explore the wreck."

He looked out the open hatch and immediately noticed that the flight bay was brilliantly lit. He could see several technicians coming over toward the shuttle. They were probably going to check out its systems after the flight to Earth and back.

"Hard to believe there are so many," Greg replied with a nod. Jason and he had spent over four weeks alone on the Moon after their lunar lander had crashed. It was something Greg hoped he would never experience again.

The two walked down the ramp and came to a stop, looking over at the second shuttle. Several technicians had two panels open on the side of the shuttle and were peering inside. One of the men seemed to be making adjustments or repairs to something.

"I hope they know what they're doing," muttered Greg, shaking his head with his eyes focused on the technicians. "The Federation's technology is a lot further along than ours."

"I'm sure Ariel is helping them," Jason reassured Greg. "Let's get to the conference room and see what's been going on since we left."

They passed through the double airlock and started down the short corridor, passing through the hatch. As they walked through the ship, one of the first things they noticed was that all the lights were on. Evidently, all the broken ones had been replaced. Even more surprising was that all the wreckage had been cleared from the corridors. In several areas, large metal patches had been welded into place to strengthen the walls.

"They've done a lot of work up here," Greg noted as they passed several technicians carrying their tools and other equipment. "From inside here it's hard to believe we're in a crashed spaceship."

"If not for the outside, you wouldn't know this ship is a wreck," agreed Jason as they stepped through another hatch. This section of the Avenger had survived relatively intact.

A few minutes later, they reached the conference room and after knocking, went inside. Colonel Greene, Lisa Gordon, Adam Simmins, and another man and woman they weren't familiar with were sitting at the long conference table.

"Commander Strong and Greg; it's good to see you again," spoke Colonel Greene, standing up and walking over to meet the two men. He shook both of their hands before continuing. "I think you know everyone except Karl Stern and Andrea Oleson. Karl is a physicist and has several other science degrees. Andrea is a doctor and highly familiar with most of the strains of flu that have existed in recent years, including the Spanish Flu."

"Hello, Commander Strong," a pleasant feminine voice spoke from the front of the conference room. "Nice to see you again, Greg. I am excited that you agreed to come with Commander Strong on this mission."

Looking up, Jason saw a large viewscreen with an image of Ariel dressed in her dark blue uniform. "Hello, Ariel."

The dark haired girl on the screen nodded and smiled. Her dark eyes showed her pleasure at Jason and Greg being in the conference room.

"If everyone will take a seat, I will go over what we know and what we hope to accomplish with this mission," Colonel Greene said.

Jason and Greg sat down and turned to face the colonel. They were both curious to hear what he was going to say. General Adamson and Tom Hays had both been a little evasive when asked specific questions about the mission. Both had said that Colonel Greene would brief them on what they hoped to accomplish if they could find and get into the Federation base on Ceres.

"As you have been told, it seems that the humans that fled to our Solar System after the destruction of the Human Federation of Worlds realized they couldn't colonize Earth."

"Because of the flu," Greg said, recalling what Ariel had told them weeks back. "Their civilian ships became infected with it."

"We don't think all of them were," Doctor Oleson spoke with a serious look upon her face. She was thirty-four years old and had made medicine and the study of diseases her life. "They made an attempt to contain it to a few ships." Doctor Oleson looked over at Lisa.

"From what we have been able to learn from Ariel there was a concentrated attempt to contain it on the civilian ships," Lisa continued. She had talked to Ariel considerably about this, trying to find out what had happened. "Once the doctors realized they couldn't stop the spread of the disease, they made a drastic decision. All the infected colonists were moved to a few ships and placed in quarantine. The doctors and scientists that remained in the fleet did everything they could to disinfect their remaining ships to stop the spread of the deadly disease."

"It was the only thing they could do," Doctor Oleson explained. "They had no immunity at all. The flu would run its course in less than 48 hours, usually resulting in death. The doctors in the fleet just didn't have the necessary facilities or the time to create an effective serum. They felt a strict quarantine was their only option."

"So some of the colonists as well as their military personnel may have survived?" asked Jason, thinking about the ramifications. "Do we have any idea how many?"

"No," replied Colonel Greene, shaking his head sadly. "We think many probably died. Their attempt to disinfect their ships probably failed in some cases. Andrea believes that as many as sixty percent of the civilians may have died before they managed to control the spread of the disease."

"That still leaves nearly 16,000 survivors out of their civilian population, plus their military," spoke Jason, recalling how many had been in the civilian refugee fleet. "Do we have any idea how many were in their military ships?"

Colonel Greene was silent for a moment. "Commander, how big do you think the Avenger was before the accident?"

Jason looked confused and then he answered. "The surviving section is about 400 feet long and 200 feet wide. I guess if you add the damaged section and the wreckage in the crater floor the ship might have been about 500 or 600 feet long." Jason noticed Ariel smiling, and Colonel Greene was shaking his head.

"You're not even close," Greene responded. He turned to Ariel and said. "Will you tell Commander Strong and Greg what the specifications are for a Human Federation of World's light cruiser?"

"A fully intact light cruiser would measure 600 meters in length, 150 meters wide, and 150 meters thick. It would have a crew of 500 with an additional complement of 75 marines. The ship would be equipped with over 80 weapon emplacements and two Shrike missile pods. It would also be equipped with two medium bow laser batteries."

"Lasers," Greg said, his eyes lighting up. This was what he had been wanting to find out. "Can I see the lasers?"

"They were destroyed in the crash," explained Colonel Greene, shaking his head. "Nearly 50 feet of the bow of the ship is imbedded in the crater wall. The other weapons Ariel is talking about are kinetic energy weapons. The ship's weapons are capable of firing large armor piercing rounds at extremely high speeds. This is far greater than anything we have ever been able to achieve. We're still looking at their missile capability. Unfortunately, most of the missiles were destroyed in the crash. We only have a few heavily damaged ones to inspect."

"This ship was nearly 2,000 feet in length," Jason spoke, astonished at the thought. "Where's the rest of it? I don't think even the wreckage out in the crater will account for that much."

"We're still searching," Colonel Greene replied. "It could be anywhere on the Moon's surface. After the explosion in Engineering, many of Ariel's sensors went off line. Commander Standel managed to get some of the ship's maneuvering thrusters working and tried to bring the ship down for a landing, but the thrusters were not powerful enough. The Avenger crashed, and most of the remaining crew were killed."

"Commander Standel," repeated Jason, recalling the mummified body they had found in the room next to the Command Center. "Was that the body we found?"

"Yes," Ariel replied sadly, with obvious pain in her voice. "He was a good commander. The Fleet Admiral thought very highly of him."

"Ariel believes that the Avenger broke apart as it came down," Lisa continued. "The added stress from the maneuvering thrusters plus the damage already done to the Engineering section caused the ship to break apart. The rocket engine you found in the crater is part of the maneuvering system, not the actual drive system for the ship. The ship broke apart just behind the flight bay. All of Engineering, the sublight drive, and the FTL core are gone."

Jason and Greg just looked at each other. If a Federation light cruiser was 2,000 feet long, how big were the first line jobs?

"So what do you want us to do at Ceres?" asked Jason, looking over at Colonel Greene. "Ceres is a pretty large asteroid. It's nearly 590 miles in diameter. It might not be that easy to find the base, especially if it's concealed."

"I don't believe that will be a problem," Ariel spoke, her dark eyes focusing on Jason. "I will furnish you with the Avenger's identification codes. I believe that if we broadcast them at Ceres, once you go into orbit the base will make itself known."

"If the base is actually there," Greg spoke with a frown. "If there is no response, we may not be able to find it."

"Assuming we find the base and can get inside, then what?" Jason asked. "What will we be looking for?"

"We don't believe there are any survivors currently alive on Ceres," Colonel Greene spoke. "I wish there were; they could teach us so much. I firmly believe if there were survivors there would be some sign."

"Have you tried contacting them?" Greg asked. Turning his head to look at Ariel, Greg continued. "Don't you have some way to contact the base now that you have power?"

"I have been trying," confessed Ariel, looking slightly guilty.

"You have?" spoke Colonel Greene, looking stunned. "I thought you agreed not to do anything without first consulting with me."

"I am truly sorry, Colonel," Ariel replied, her eyes taking on a trapped look. "But there are commands buried deep within my program, which demand that I attempt to contact the nearest Human Federation of World's base. That would be Ceres. I have been trying for over three weeks, and there has been no reply to any of my hails. I don't believe there are any survivors on Ceres." The expression of anguish and sadness on her face said more than mere words possibly could.

Jason understood her sorrow. She was the last survivor of the Human Federation of Worlds. It was times like this that Ariel seemed almost human.

"She has to comply," Lisa broke in, seeing that the colonel was getting angry. "She is only obeying her orders, just as you are."

Colonel Greene took a deep, calming breath and then nodded his head. "Very well, I guess I can understand. Ariel, since they are not replying, can you stop broadcasting?"

"Yes, Colonel Greene," Ariel replied. "In the absence of direct orders from the nearest base, my program is authorized to recognize another human as my commander. It is something I should have already done."

"Then do so," ordered Colonel Greene expecting Ariel to name him since he was the highest ranking military officer present.

Ariel closed her eyes briefly and then opened them. "It is done. Commander Jason Strong is now my new commander."

"What!" Colonel Greene spoke in a stunned voice, his eyes widening in confusion. This was not what he had wanted or expected to hear. "Why Commander Strong?"

"I trust Commander Strong. He meets all the criteria to be my new commander, even though the Avenger will never leave this moon. Commander Strong may state who his second in command will be."

Jason looked around the room. He didn't know what to say.

"You need to be careful, Jason," Lisa whispered quietly leaning over toward him. "I don't know what Ariel would do if you declined. Tell her you accept and then name Colonel Greene as your executive officer. That should get us by for now until I can speak in more detail with Ariel later."

"I accept," spoke Jason, standing up and facing Ariel. "Colonel Greene will be promoted to the position of executive officer. During my absence, you will obey all of his orders."

Colonel Greene rose and, looking over at Lisa, turned to face Ariel. He had overheard what Lisa had told Jason. "I accept the position of executive officer of the Avenger." He didn't see what other choice he had.

"Commander Strong's recommendation has been noted and recorded," Ariel replied.

"Now, since that's settled, let's finish our briefing," said Jason, sitting back down and looking over at Colonel Green. He still felt strange about taking over as commander of a crashed warship. "What do we do if we get inside the base?"

"We want to see if any of their warships are still intact," Greene responded in a serious tone. "We have one in particular we want you to look for. It's the light cruiser Vindication."

"Why the Vindication?" Greg asked. "What's so special about it?"

He still couldn't believe that Ariel had promoted Jason over Colonel Greene. This day was full of surprises. The AI had them over a barrel. He knew they couldn't object. They needed the AI and the technical information she had in her memory banks.

"It's actually quite simple," responded Colonel Greene, cocking his eyebrow. "The Vindication has an AI named Clarissa on board. We want you to activate her and then, if it's feasible, bring the Vindication back to the Moon."

"What!" Greg stammered, his eyes growing wide in disbelief. "You want us to fly a 2,000 foot warship back to the Moon?"

"There will only be eight of us," Jason reminded the colonel. "I don't believe eight people are enough to do that. Just manning the Command Center would take a larger group, not to mention Engineering and the other essential sections of the ship."

"It should be possible if Clarissa is still sentient," Ariel replied with hope in her voice as she took over the conversation. "I will give you the command codes, which will clear you with her security systems. Clarissa, once she is brought back to full operational status, will be able to ascertain if the Vindication is capable of making the flight back to the Moon. With the absence of her crew, Clarissa is capable of flying the ship and operating all of the Vindication's systems on her own. You will just be passengers enjoying the ride."

Jason shook his head in disbelief. He couldn't believe what they were asking him and Greg to do. He leaned back and closed his eyes. This mission had just gotten a lot more complicated. He wondered what was next.

Jason was walking down a corridor searching for Greg. Lisa had told him that Greg had gone off to inspect the ship's railguns. This didn't surprise Jason at all. He knew how curious Greg was about the Avenger's armaments. Ariel had finally agreed to give them access to the weapon systems several weeks previously. Several experts had already flown up from Earth to begin examining the advanced weapons the ship was equipped with.

After talking to several technicians who were working in this section of the ship, they indicated which direction Greg had gone. After a few more minutes of searching, Jason found an open hatch that led to one of the railgun turrets. Stepping inside, he found himself in a small room. Greg was hovering over what looked like a large, double-barreled cannon that occupied much of the space.

"So that's a railgun," commented Jason, walking over to stand next to Greg and eyeing the railgun.

"Jason," Greg responded with a big grin. "Look what I found!"

Jason could tell that Greg was genuinely excited at getting to examine this advanced weapon of the Federation. "We have those down on Earth," Jason said. He had been fortunate to see several railgun demonstrations a few years earlier.

"Not like these," replied Greg, running his hand along one of the large barrels of the railgun. "I measured this thing and it's capable of hurling 60 mm projectiles. From what Ariel told me, these were used to destroy inbound missiles and enemy fighters. The ship was originally equipped with 48 of these twin railgun turrets."

"That's not a very big round," Jason responded as he looked closer at the railgun. He had expected something much larger and more destructive. He noticed the railgun was on a platform that could be extended until the turret projected from the hull of the ship.

"Big enough," responded Greg, stepping back and looking down the length of one of the barrels. He had measured it earlier, and it was slightly over ten feet long. "Ariel said these were called defensive turrets and could fire five rounds every second. Since they're double cannons, that's ten rounds a second or 600 rounds per minute. At the speed the rounds were fired, that's a lot of punishing power. Enough to destroy an inbound missile or a fighter."

Jason nodded; he could well understand how useful these defensive turrets could be in a battle. They could protect the ship from incoming missiles and attacking fighters while the big guns concentrated on their main targets.

"Have you looked at any of the big turrets?" Jason asked, curiously. He knew the Avenger had a number of much larger railguns.

Greg grinned like a kid who had just gotten his first puppy. "Just down the corridor and up one flight of stairs is a larger one. It's a secondary offensive railgun. It's four times the size of this one. If you want to see something truly amazing, there is an access hatch open to one of the upper hull primary railgun batteries. That thing can fire a shell nearly a meter in diameter. Whoever designed these ships obviously knew what they were doing."

"Perhaps," Jason replied with a worried frown crossing his face. "But they lost to the Hocklyns. Evidently the weapons of the Federation weren't powerful enough to save them from defeat."

Greg was silent for a moment as he mulled that over, then he responded. "We have 268 years before they reach us. Maybe by then our weapons will be better."

"I guess all that depends on what we find on Ceres. If there are intact ships inside the asteroid, it could save us years of research. Even with Ariel's help, it's going to be a bitch to build a ship like the Avenger."

Greg nodded. He looked back at the twin railgun. It was a masterful piece of equipment and engineering. Perhaps sometime in the future, his son would fly in a ship such as this. Greg let out a deep breath. It was just dawning on him how important this mission was.

"Don't forget, we have flight training in the morning," Jason reminded Greg. He was looking forward to learning how to fly one of the shuttles. "We have a lot to learn before we're ready to go to Ceres."

Jason and Greg were in a small room just across from the flight bay. Lieutenant Addison, the young pilot that had sat in the pilot's seat when the shuttle had brought Jason and Greg to the Moon, was explaining to them how the simulator worked.

"There were half a dozen simulators in this room to begin with," he explained, pointing at a number of partially disassembled machines. "Ariel had the technicians cannibalize parts from the others to get this one functioning."

"How does it work?" asked Jason, looking with interest at the simulator. There were two seats in front of him with what looked like a flight helmet with a full visor on the front hanging above them. This wasn't like any simulator he had ever used before.

"It's virtual reality," explained Addison, grinning. "Put the helmet on, and a virtual world is created which mimics the inside of the cockpit for the shuttle. We don't really understand how it works, but everything seems extremely real."

Jason looked over at Greg and then, shrugging his shoulders, sat down in the indicated chair for the pilot. Greg sat down in the other.

"You're sure this thing is safe?" asked Greg, glancing uneasily at the lieutenant.

Lieutenant Addison laughed and nodded his head. "I've used it dozens of times over the past four weeks. It's perfectly safe."

Greg tried to relax. He wondered how this would work.

Lieutenant Addison stepped over and lowered the helmets, making sure they were in place. He then stepped up to the control console in front of them. Then, looking back at the two, he said. "Okay, get ready to be amazed." The lieutenant flipped several switches and pushed a large green button.

For a moment, Jason thought nothing had changed. Then, looking around, he realized that his surroundings were different, and he was no longer in the simulator room. He was sitting in the cockpit of a shuttle. Looking over to his side, he saw Greg sitting in the copilot's seat looking equally surprised.

"This is interesting," spoke Greg, looking around in amazement. "How the hell can they do this? Everything looks so real."

"If you two are ready, we will begin the instrument familiarization part of this simulation," Lieutenant Addison spoke. His voice seemed to come from a speaker that was on the console in front of them.

Looking over at Greg, Jason nodded. "Let's do it."

Jason was sitting in what at one time had been the officer's mess. Lisa Gordon and Adam Timmons were sitting across from him. They were eating a simple meal of sandwiches, chips, and sodas. A few others were at other tables eating and discussing their current projects.

"What do you two think about this mission?" asked Jason, eyeing the two.

This was the first time he had been able to get together with Lisa and Adam to discuss the trip to Ceres. He highly valued their opinions. From his time with them on the Avenger before he and Greg returned to Earth, he had gotten to know both of them quite well. They were both highly intelligent and capable of thinking outside the box. He was glad they were both going on this mission; their expertise could be quite valuable.

Lisa took a sip of her drink and then with her right hand moved a strand of blonde hair from in front of her eyes. She had let her hair grow out some since the Avenger had initiated its artificial gravity field. "I've spoken to Ariel about what she thinks we may find. The fleet had two large colony ships with them that were capable of building almost anything they wanted."

"Colony ships?" Jason asked, his eyes focusing on Lisa. "Any idea how big they were?"

"Ariel says the colony ships were nearly 2,000 meters," Lisa replied, her blue eyes studying Jason waiting for his response.

"Two thousand meters," Jason repeated slowly, his eyes growing wide. "That's three times larger than the Avenger!"

Jason leaned back in his chair and thought about what Lisa had just said. He could scarcely imagine a ship that large. The technology to build such a ship was so far in advance of anything Earth was capable of. It made Earth's space program look like a joke.

"Yes, it is," Lisa responded. Then she smiled. "The colony ships were capable of setting up a complete colony. They had numerous manufacturing systems on board which could build almost anything the colonists wanted."

"What kind of base does Ariel think they were going to build in the asteroid?" Jason asked.

The more information he could find out about the goals of the Federation survivors, the better the mission would go. He was still trying to come to grips with the technology available to the Federation. He still found it nearly incomprehensible that the Federation had lost to the Hocklyns. It made him realize even more just how dangerous the Hocklyns were.

Lisa looked over at Adam. They had discussed this already. "It would have been massive, Commander. The base they had planned originally would have been capable of housing over 100,000 people, plus all of their ships."

"That's big," responded Jason, trying to imagine a facility that large inside the asteroid.

"Perhaps larger," continued Lisa, smiling mysteriously. "The base was to be a military one and would contain all the facilities necessary to repair damaged warships as well as build new ones."

"Build new ones!" repeated Jason, drawing in a sharp breath. "How's that possible?" A facility like that would be a Godsend for Earth if it were still intact.

"You have to remember," Adam said, leaning back and laying his sandwich down on his plate. "Their science in most areas was far ahead of ours. What we would consider impossible, they would consider to be routine. Many of their construction operations were totally automated."

Jason looked at the two, thinking about what they had just said. He also remembered what his sister had said before he left about not taking any unnecessary risks. Going into a large unknown military base might be extremely dangerous. There was a good chance a base such as this, if it had actually been built, might have some type of automated defenses.

"Lisa, I need you to talk to Ariel about what type of automated defenses this base might possess, and what we can do to turn them off if we need to."

"Automated defenses," Lisa said with shock on her face.

"Damn!" Adam spoke, his eyes growing wide. "We never thought about that, but it makes sense."

"I will talk to Ariel," Lisa replied, her face turning slightly pale. She had never thought about automated defenses. None of them had.

-

One week later, Jason and Greg were going through their final flight simulation. They were in the process of landing the shuttle on the Avenger. Only in the simulation, the Avenger was in space, and they were coming in at a high speed. Jason carefully adjusted the controls and watched as the Avenger's flight bay doors slid open. Adjusting several flight controls and decreasing their speed, he brought the shuttle into the bay and landed.

"We made it," Greg spoke with a relieved smile. The first few times they had tried this simulation they had crashed into the ship. According to Lieutenant Addison, they had only died twelve times in the last ten days.

"Not bad," Lieutenant Addison said with a smile as he shut everything down. "I think I've died over 50 times in all the scenarios I've run."

"We leave tomorrow," said Jason standing up, feeling pleased with the landing. In many ways, the flight simulator had reminded him of the days he had been a military test pilot. He looked over at the young lieutenant. "Are you ready?"

Lieutenant Addison smiled and nodded his head. He would be operating the shuttle's scanners and sensors on their trip to Ceres. "I'm ready and excited. Just imagine what we might find."

"Don't get your hopes up too high, Lieutenant," cautioned Jason, understanding the young man's enthusiasm for this mission. "We don't yet know if there is anything on or in Ceres."

"Perhaps not," Addison replied, his eyes focusing on Jason. "But we won't know until we go there."

Greg just shook his head. He wondered if he had been that enthusiastic when he was the same age as Addison. "I'm going to go call Elizabeth," he said, nodding at Jason. "You should probably give Katherine and Trevor a call also. We don't know when we will be able to talk to them again."

"You're right," replied Jason, thinking about his overly protective sister. At least Katherine was still talking to him. She had been highly upset when he had told her that he was leaving again.

They left the flight simulator room knowing the next day would be big. The mission to Ceres was due to launch in the morning. Ceres was currently 262 million miles from Earth. The flight would take a little over 72 hours for the shuttle. Ariel had told them that they could do a micro-jump once they cleared the Earth and Moon's gravity well, but she didn't recommend it due to the age of the shuttle. The small craft's FTL drive was one of the few things she couldn't explain to the technicians how to properly repair or check. They would have to depend on the shuttle's sublight drive. Ariel had assured them the drive would function properly. Jason and Greg both hoped the AI was right.

Chapter Two

Jason and Greg were strapped into their acceleration couches on the shuttle, watching the control consoles in front of them. Lieutenant Addison was sitting behind them, in front of the console that controlled the shuttle's scanners and sensors. The rest of their mission crew were in the passenger compartment waiting anxiously for the launch. Ariel would control the launch and would be flying the shuttle by remote control. It was hoped that she would be able to do this all the way to Ceres.

Even though Jason was used to computers being in partial control on space missions, he still preferred the hands on approach. Of course, Ariel couldn't really be classified as a computer. Her avatar was absolutely gorgeous, and she seemed almost human if you spent any time talking to her.

"Launch in one minute, Commander," Ariel spoke calmly over the com system. "All systems read normal."

"Thank you, Ariel," replied Jason, taking a deep breath.

He wanted to fly the shuttle out himself, but he knew it was better to let Ariel handle it. Perhaps someday he would get the opportunity to fly the shuttle without computer control. In some ways, he truly missed his old days as a test pilot.

"Here we go," spoke Greg, looking over at Jason with a nervous grin. "We're going to go farther than anyone from our world has ever gone before. I just hope we make it back."

Greg had spoken to his wife for quite some time the previous night. If everything went as they hoped, this mission wouldn't last more than a few weeks and he would be safely back home with his family. He was already missing holding his son and being with his wife.

Jason heard the shuttle's engines increase slightly in pitch and knew it was time. He watched the flight controls, ready to take over at a moments notice if there were any signs of trouble. His heartbeat quickened. He took a deep breath and then slowly let it out.

The shuttle rose above the deck in the flight bay and flew smoothly out the large double door. It made a slight popping noise as it passed through the atmospheric force field. Ariel sent the shuttle up at a gentle angle and slowly accelerated the small ship. For twenty minutes, the speed of the shuttle increased until it was moving at slightly over 1,000 miles per second. Ariel knew that, at this speed, they would rendezvous with Ceres in a little over 76 hours. The mission was on its way. Everything had gone smoothly with the launch, just as she had expected. She did a quick scan of the shuttle's systems and saw that everything was functioning smoothly. Perhaps in a few more days, she would know if Clarissa had survived. She hoped so, it would be wonderful to have another AI to talk to.

"All systems are functioning normally, Commander," Ariel reported. The shuttle had enough redundancy built into it that she wasn't concerned about a minor system failure. "Shuttle is on the planned flight path."

"Thank you, Ariel," replied Jason, allowing himself to relax. "That was a very smooth launch."

Jason looked over the controls on the console in front of him. There were several screens that showed the current status of the ship's systems. All of these showed normal as Ariel had said. A slightly larger screen in the center of the console showed the shuttle's planned course. To the right of the large screen was a smaller one that showed what the scanners were picking up in the shuttle's immediate vicinity.

Behind Jason, Lieutenant Addison was watching his own screens, which showed everything within 100,000 miles of the shuttle. "All screens are clear," he reported as he leaned forward and entered some information on the computer in front of him. At the speed they were traveling, if something did show up on the scanners or the long-range sensors they would only have 100 seconds to react to it.

Greg looked out the cockpit window, mesmerized by the sight. The Earth was visible, and the friendly blue-white globe was slowly shrinking as the shuttle sped away from it. He was leaving his wife and child behind and embarking on a journey the likes of which no one on the planet below had even thought possible. He also knew they were traveling faster than any human from Earth had ever traveled before. They were on their way to Ceres and, with luck, he would see sights that no one else ever had. This was why he had joined the private space program and embarked on the New Beginnings mission. Now he was in space again on a new mission of discovery.

"We'll be back," spoke Jason, looking over at Greg and seeing him looking at the planet below. "Your wife and son will be waiting."

"I know," Greg replied softly, finding the spot on the shrinking globe where his family was. "We had a good talk last night. She just worries when I'm gone."

"You have a good wife," Jason added with a smile. "I talked to Katherine last night also. She's still not happy with my decision to take on this mission."

"At least she's still talking to you," Greg commented. Even though he was going to miss his family, he was glad he had made the decision to come on this mission.

Jason nodded; he hated upsetting his sister. However, this was the career that he had chosen. It had started with him becoming a test pilot, then working for the private space company that had launched the New Beginnings mission, and now for the government flying this mission to Ceres.

Lisa poked her head into the cockpit and looked nervously around. "I guess we're on our way." She wasn't used to space travel. Her only trip into space so far had been on the lunar lander that had landed on the Moon after Jason and Greg had crashed.

"Everything looks good here," spoke Jason, nodding at Lisa with a reassuring smile. "Next stop should be Ceres."

"Don't worry, Lisa," Ariel's calm voice came over the com system. "This should be a smooth flight, and we're going at a speed that will not put any stress on the shuttle's systems."

"How fast can this shuttle go?" Greg asked, curiously. In the simulator, they had flown the shuttle at speeds in excess of 2,000 miles per second.

"Maximum speed for the shuttle is 4,000 miles per second," Ariel answered in a calm voice. "Normally the shuttle would use its sublight drive to travel out of a planet or moon's gravity well and then perform a short micro-jump to its destination."

"Any idea what we might be facing in the way of defenses once we arrive at Ceres?" Jason asked. He had requested that Lisa talk this over with Ariel to see if the shuttle could be in danger from any automatic defenses the Federation survivors might have installed years in the past.

"Ariel, tell Commander Strong about the possible defenses that might surround this base we're going to," Lisa requested.

She had spent a lot of time going over this with Ariel and asking questions. Some of Ariel's replies had been quite disturbing. This mission might be a lot more dangerous than they had originally thought.

For a moment, nothing came over the com system. Then finally, Ariel spoke. "Lisa has a data disk which describes in detail the possible defensive systems that might exist around and inside of Ceres."

"What might we be facing if the base is indeed intact and fully operational?" Jason asked. From all the scans and observations that had been made there were no signs the base had ever been built. However, Jason was not willing to take any chances.

"Tell him, Ariel," Lisa spoke, her eyes looking out the viewports at the stars. The view was breathtaking. "We can go over the disk and more details later. Just give the commander a general idea of what we may be facing."

"Orbital missile platforms, railgun platforms, and even high intensity lasers will be the biggest threat," Ariel replied in an even voice. "My guess would be that some weapon placements might be embedded in nearby asteroids to reduce their chance of discovery."

"How do we get past those?" Greg asked, uneasily. It sounded as if they might be blown out of space before they even got near the asteroid.

"Once the shuttle gets within range of Ceres, I will begin transmitting the Avenger's identification codes," Ariel responded in a confident voice. "The codes should allow the shuttle to pass safely through any exterior defenses that might exist. The weapons will not fire on a Federation vessel. The defenses, if they exist, were designed to fire on a Hocklyn vessel."

"What about once we reach the asteroid?" Jason asked, his forehead creasing in a frown. He knew there were bound to be some interior defenses as well. "Will there be defenses inside the asteroid also?"

"I don't believe the interior defenses will fire upon a human," Ariel replied in a more hesitant voice. "They would have been designed to repel an invading Hocklyn force. Their version of our marines are called protectors."

"But you're not sure, are you?" asked Jason, noticing the AI's hesitation.

"No," Ariel admitted in a voice that sounded a lot less certain. "The interior defenses will be controlled by the base's computer. It should recognize you as human. Once inside the base, you will be carrying a communication device, which will continue to broadcast the Avenger's identification codes. Those codes should allow you to proceed deep into the base until you can make contact with the base's computer."

"That's a lot of ifs," Greg complained with a heavy frown. It sounded to him as if Ariel wasn't that sure about what would happen once they got inside.

"If you can get inside the base, I can use the communication device to speak to the installation's computer. Once I identify myself, there should not be any problems."

"Let's hope not," Jason said. "We all want to come back home."

He had spoken in great detail with Colonel Greene about this mission. Colonel Greene had made it extremely clear how important this mission was. In order for the Earth to be ready to face the Hocklyns in 268 years, they needed every advantage they could find. An intact Federation base would be a huge step in the right direction. It could save them years or even decades of research.

It had been 48 hours since the shuttle had left the Moon. Greg was gazing out the cockpit window at the stars, deep in thought. If their mission was a success and his son followed in his father's footsteps, then someday he might get to travel to one of those unblinking specks of light. Around some of those stars would be planets waiting for people from Earth to plant colonies on and grow into powerful allies of Earth. Someday those colonies and Earth would face the Hocklyns. On that day, it would be decided whether humanity would be free or become part of the Slaver Empire. In some ways, Greg was glad that he wouldn't be around to see what happened.

"Shuttle is still on course and all systems are functioning normally," Ariel reported over the com system. She was tied into the shuttle's computer and was constantly monitoring the shuttle as it flew through space toward Ceres.

"Ariel," Greg began, still thinking about the Hocklyns. "What do you think the odds are of Earth being able to survive when the Hocklyns arrive?"

Ariel was silent for a moment. This wasn't the first time she had been asked that question. "There are a number of possibilities. By the time the Hocklyns reach Earth, there is a very good possibility that Earth will have a powerful space fleet. At least comparable to what the Federation had. In the case of Earth, we know the Hocklyns are coming and what has to be done. We have 268 years to prepare. The Federation had less than a year."

Greg leaned back and closed his eyes. He noticed that Ariel had used the term we. That was encouraging. If this base on Ceres was a bust, at least they still had Ariel and her knowledge. This was a war he would never see or take part in, but he knew it would occupy the rest of his life. He let out a deep breath and opened his eyes gazing out at the stars. It was difficult to imagine the danger they hid. For years, he had watched the distant stars and dreamed of flying to them. Now they hid a menace, which could wipe out the human race.

Jason was back in the passenger compartment talking to the rest of the team. He wanted everyone to be ready for whatever they might face once they reached the asteroid. He had already gone over in detail the possible defenses they might run into. Earlier he had covered the data disk that Lisa had. His face had gotten pale when he realized the extent of the defenses they might be facing. Lisa was currently briefing the others on what the base might be like.

"According to Ariel, this base could be immense," explained Lisa, looking around the group. "If they were able to finish it, the base would be capable of supporting over 100,000 people and would have repair bays for all of their major warships. There would also be bays for the other ships that were with them. If they had enough time, the base was to be expanded to contain full construction bays capable of building any Federation warship."

"How could they build such a large base?" Professor Stern asked with doubt in his voice. He found it incomprehensible that the humans in the refugee fleet could have built the base Lisa was describing. An undertaking such as that would have taken years, possibly decades. "Surely they all died out from the flu before much work could be done or we would have heard from them. It's more likely that all we will find is a partially built base and perhaps some of their ships with their dead still inside."

"They had a work robot that resembled a large spider," responded Lisa, shaking her head at Professor Stern. She opened a folder and handed Karl a picture that she had downloaded from Ariel. "They were about six feet long and could be programmed to do almost any type of construction job, including building warships."

"Mean looking suckers," mumbled Professor Stern, looking at the picture and then passing it on. "They do resemble giant spiders. But I still don't believe they could have built this base."

"And they had these in the evacuation fleet?" asked Marvin Tennyson, looking over at Lisa. Marvin was an astrophysicist and extremely knowledgeable about the geography of the Solar System and the asteroids.

"The colony ships had them," Lisa answered with a nod. "They would have been used to do the majority of the work setting up a new colony. They could also have been used to help build the base." She looked over at Professor Stern, whose expression still showed the faintest hint of skepticism.

"If the base is there, it's possible we might encounter some of these construction robots," Jason informed the group, looking around at each one. "If all the humans died out due to the flu, the robots might have been tasked with finishing the base and then maintaining it. At least that's what we're hoping. It might also explain why we haven't heard anything from the base."

"How dangerous is it going to be to approach Ceres?" asked Adam, folding his arms across his chest. "Won't we be in danger of hitting other asteroids as we get closer to our destination?"

"Even in the area of space where Ceres is located, asteroids are few and far between," Tennyson answered. "The asteroids are the remains of a planet that never formed in our Solar System. They exist in a ring between Mars and Jupiter but never coalesced into a planet. Ceres is the largest and, according to some of my colleagues, is considered to be a dwarf planet."

The meeting lasted for another hour, and then everyone retired to get some rest. The interior of the shuttle had been remodeled and large, comfortable acceleration couches had been installed that could be reclined to allow the crew to sleep in relative comfort. Food and water were contained in storage bins in one wall, and there were several microwaves to heat their food. The shuttle had enough food and water to last the mission for several weeks if it became necessary.

It was a little over 26 hours later and everyone was feeling nervous. The shuttle was nearing Ceres, and Ariel had already started broadcasting the Avenger's identification codes toward the asteroid. Lieutenant Addison was watching his scanner and sensor screens, which now showed the asteroid as well as numerous other small asteroids in close proximity to Ceres.

"Why are there so many small asteroids around Ceres?" asked Addison, feeling perplexed. He hadn't expected to find so many. After speaking to Marvin Tennyson, he had expected Ceres to be the only asteroid on his screens.

"It doesn't make any sense," Tennyson replied as he gazed in confusion at the scanner screen. It showed over 50 small asteroids within 200 miles of Ceres. Most ranged from 100 to 300 feet in diameter. "Ceres own small gravity field should have cleared these out years ago. From watching the scans, it seems as if these asteroids are in orbit around Ceres. That's impossible."

"Not if they're disguised weapons platforms," Ariel commented over the com system. The small orbiting asteroids had been a surprise to her also.

"Weapons platforms!" Greg spoke with alarm in his voice. He had hoped there wouldn't be any. "Could they still be functional after all of these years?"

"Possibly," replied Ariel, sounding a little tense. "The Avenger's identification codes I'm broadcasting should stop them from firing on the shuttle. These small asteroids may be proof that the base was indeed built."

"If they do fire, can we avoid the incoming ordinance?" asked Jason, eyeing the controls in front of him. The shuttle wasn't a fighter jet or one of the high performance space fighters that used to be in the Avenger's flight bay.

"No," Ariel replied in an even voice. "As long as we continue broadcasting and do not show any aggressive moves, the shuttle should be fine."

"That's easy for you to say," commented Greg, shaking his head dubiously. "You're safe on the Avenger."

Jason glanced at the scanner screen on the main flight console in front of him. It was now covered with blips indicating the numerous asteroids they were nearing. He watched as Ariel adjusted and plotted a new course which should take them safely through. Tension crept into his shoulders as they continued to approach what might be Federation weapons platforms.

"New course plotted," Ariel reported after a moment. "I'm putting the shuttle on a course that will stay as far away from the possible weapons platforms as possible."

"I want everyone to get into their acceleration couches and be prepared for some violent maneuvers if we're fired upon," Jason ordered.

Ariel remained silent. She knew if the platforms fired, the shuttle would be destroyed. The interceptor missiles from the Federation were quite accurate and fast. The shuttle would never be able to get away in time.

"Ariel, have you detected any type of response at all from the base?" asked Jason, his eyes focused intently on the scanner screen. He had hoped once they began broadcasting the Avenger's codes that there would be some type of reaction.

"No, Commander," Ariel replied in an uneasy voice. She was beginning to wonder if this mission had been a mistake. "I had hoped for a response from the codes, but so far there has been nothing. I will continue to observe and let you know if there are any changes."

Greg looked over at Jason, shaking his head. "I don't like this, Jason. If even one of those platforms fires, this shuttle won't stand much of a chance."

"I know," responded Jason, glancing uneasily out the cockpit window. The asteroids weren't visible, but he knew they were there. "Lieutenant Addison, keep a close watch on the scanner screen. Greg, make sure we continue to broadcast the Avenger's identification codes." Jason returned his gaze to the scanner screen and the numerous contacts it was showing.

Greg leaned forward and checked the com system. Ariel was still broadcasting the codes, but there was still no response from Ceres. "Maybe the base's computer has failed," Greg suggested. Looking out the cockpit window, he could barely see Ceres. Out this far from the sun, there wasn't much sunlight.

The shuttle continued its cautious approach. It would pass uncomfortably close to several of the asteroids even on its new course. From the asteroids, targeting sensors reached out and scanned the approaching shuttle. Weapons locked on and prepared to fire. No one on the shuttle was aware that they were being tracked by numerous railgun and missile platforms, any of which could blow the fragile shuttle out of space in an instant. Computers in the emplacements picked up the friendly broadcast of a Federation ship's ID code and held their fire. Only a direct order from their command base could override the platform's computers. The shuttle would be allowed to pass. Even so, the weapons continued to track the shuttle in case the base's computer ordered them to fire.

Ariel picked up the targeting scans but decided it was best not to mention it to Jason. She had been expecting and hoping for this. No need to worry the crew about something they were powerless to prevent. The shuttle's scanners and sensors remained clear of incoming ordinance, so the broadcast of the Avenger's codes must be working. The targeting scans she had picked up proved that at least part of the Federation base must have been built. Ariel hoped that the Vindication was inside the asteroid. She would love to talk to Clarissa, the Vindication's AI.

Long minutes passed. The shuttle continued to slow and finally came to a stop twenty miles from the massive asteroid. On the shuttle's main viewscreen, a jagged desolate surface was revealed. The surface of Ceres was pockmarked with numerous small asteroid strikes. In many ways, it resembled the surface of the Moon.

"Any recommendations?" Jason asked as he looked out the cockpit window at the looming asteroid. "There has been no response to our signals, and I don't see any way to knock on the door to let them know we're here."

"Hold position, Commander," Ariel replied. "I am now sending a more detailed explanation as to why we are here. I am hoping this will elicit a response from the base."

Moments later, a loud squealing noise came over the com system. At the same instant, all the lights in the shuttle flickered, and the scanner and sensor screens went blank.

"Ariel, what just happened?" Jason demanded with concern growing on his face. Were they under attack? For several moments he waited, but Ariel didn't answer. "Ariel, are you still receiving us?"

"She's not going to answer," Lieutenant Addison spoke with a worried frown on this face. "There's some type of jamming that is affecting all outgoing and incoming communication. It's also blocking our scanners and sensors."

"So we're effectively blind," said Greg, looking uncomfortably out the cockpit window at the asteroid. He felt a cold chills running down his neck as he realized how vulnerable the shuttle was. He could imagine railguns and lasers targeting the shuttle and preparing to fire.

"Yes," replied Addison, working frantically on the touch screen on his console. He stopped and looked at Jason. "There's nothing I can do from here."

"At least we know the base is there and it's active," commented Jason, letting out a sharp breath. His eyes turned back toward the asteroid. Nothing had changed.

"What do we do now?" asked Greg, glancing over at Jason. "We can't even attempt to talk to them if our communications are being jammed. We could use the manual flight controls and attempt to land."

"Yes, but land where? That asteroid has more land area than the state of Texas."

"Sir, if I am not mistaken there are new commands being transmitted to our flight computer," Addison spoke nervously as he watched a screen on his console. "I don't think Ariel is in control of the shuttle any longer. These commands are not coming from Ariel."

As if to prove the lieutenant correct, the shuttle began to move slowly toward the asteroid. Down on the asteroid's surface, a disguised hatch slid open and lights inside flicked on, illuminating a landing bay.

"I guess we're being invited in," Jason said, letting out a sharp breath. Suddenly the situation had been taken completely out of their control. "This base is a lot more active than what Ariel thought it would be."

"But who has taken control of our shuttle?" asked Greg uneasily as he looked out the cockpit window at the landing bay they were approaching. He had a nervous and worried look on his face. "Are there people down there, or is this being done by a computer like Ariel? She said there was one on the Vindication. Could Clarissa be in charge of the base?"

"I don't know," replied Jason, trying to sound calm. He was just glad his sister didn't know what was happening. This was just the type of danger she had warned him about.

"Addison, go get Lisa, maybe she can shed some light on this," Jason ordered. Looking out the cockpit window, he saw the shuttle was nearing the opening of the lighted landing bay in the asteroid. In a few more minutes, they would be inside.

A few moments later, Lisa arrived in the cockpit and looking out the cockpit window, her eyes widened in surprise. "So the broadcast must have worked. That's the base!"

"In a way," Jason replied in a steady voice. "We have lost contact with Ariel and have no control over the shuttle. We're being flown into that landing bay ahead by remote control."

Lisa was silent as she mulled over what Jason had just said. "We were not expecting anything like this. I don't know what to tell you other than we don't want to resist or do anything that might be construed as being threatening. If this is a computer that is in control, it might consider any such move as justification to destroy the shuttle. Remember, this is supposed to be a military base."

"That's just great," muttered Greg, rubbing his forehead in exasperation. "This just gets better every minute."

"No one said this trip was going to be boring," Jason reminded him with a forced smile.

"It's definitely not boring," Greg replied with an agreeing nod. Looking ahead, he tried to peer into the landing bay, but he still couldn't see anything.

Everyone in the cockpit continued to watch as the shuttle was finally maneuvered into the landing bay. The shuttle landed gently on the deck and, as soon as it was down, the doors to the landing bay slid shut, sealing them in.

"Interference has stopped," reported Lieutenant Addison seeing all of his screens return to normal.

"Don't send any messages or attempt to scan our surroundings," Lisa warned, her blue eyes boring into Lieutenant Addison. "Shut the sensors and scanners down."

Addison looked at Jason. "Do as she says, Lieutenant," Jason ordered. He trusted Lisa's judgment. After all, she was the computer expert. "What do you suggest, Lisa?"

"I think we should wait inside the shuttle and see if we're contacted. If nothing happens, then we can send the Avenger's ID codes one more time with a question as to what we are expected to do. The message should mention that we have valuable information for the base. That should elicit a response from the computer that's in control."

"Do you think it's Clarissa?" asked Jason, wondering if the Vindication's AI was doing this.

"I don't know," Lisa replied slowly. "I would have thought Clarissa would have responded to Ariel."

"Then I guess we wait," spoke Jason, taking a deep breath.

Looking out the cockpit window, he could see they were inside a large landing bay similar to the flight bay back on the Avenger. Only this one was about ten times that size. Over to one side were parked several more shuttles, and as he continued to gaze around he could see over a dozen space fighters parked over next to one wall.

"Do you see those fighters, Jason?" Greg asked, his eyes lighting up with excitement. "They look completely intact! I hope we get a chance to look them over."

"Lisa, is there any possibility of there being survivors still inside this base?" Jason asked. From what he could see and what had happened so far, he couldn't imagine a computer doing all of this. There had to be humans involved somewhere.

"According to Doctor Oleson, there is a slim possibility. If they were successful in quarantining everyone that had flu like symptoms, they had the doctors and medical research staff to eventually perfect a vaccine. They could have survived. But if they did, why haven't they contacted us before now?"

"I don't know," Jason replied. "I guess we will find out shortly."

For 30 heart-stopping minutes, they waited. There were no incoming messages from the base, and Ariel was still silent. Evidently, something in the material used to construct the base prevented communication signals from entering and exiting. Jason had everyone go to the passenger compartment so they could decide what to do next.

"I guess we go out," Jason said, looking around the small group. "Lieutenant Addison, you and Professor Tennyson will stay inside the shuttle. I want someone here in case the base attempts to make contact. The rest of us will go into the base and see what we can find. It's looking to me like a computer is in charge. If there were people here, we should have seen an armed welcoming committee by now. I can't imagine a military base allowing a strange shuttle to land in their landing bay and not responding to it."

"I agree, Commander," Lisa commented with a nod. "I don't think it's Clarissa either. If it were the Vindication's AI, she would have contacted us. This may indeed be the base's computer, and it may well be acting on a predetermined set of protocols."

"Then I guess we go out and introduce ourselves to this computer," Jason replied.

A few minutes later, the small group of six walked down the shuttle's extended ramp. Once they were down, Jason signaled Lieutenant Addison. The ramp slid back into the shuttle and the hatch closed. They were all wearing tan spacesuits from the Avenger. They were lightweight and much more comfortable than the bulky NASA spacesuits they were all so familiar with.

"We have artificial gravity," spoke Greg, realizing that his weight felt normal.

Greg's eyes swept across the bay expecting to see a welcoming committee appear at any moment, but the bay remained empty of movement. His eyes lingered on the space fighters. He would really like to go over and check them out, but now was not the time. Perhaps later there would be a better opportunity.

"There's a hatch over on that wall," commented Adam, pointing toward it. "We should be able to get out of the landing bay from there."

"Let's see what's behind it," said Jason.

Reaching the hatch Jason attempted to open it, but it wouldn't budge. Turning to look at Lisa, he asked. "Any ideas?" He didn't like the idea of being trapped in the bay. They were too exposed.

"Just a moment," replied Lisa, turning on a small data pad she was carrying in her right hand. She skimmed through several pages of data until she found what she wanted. She then stepped over to a small key pad on the wall next to the hatch and entered a series of numbers. Like magic, the hatch opened with a slight hissing noise. "Ariel gave me some command codes that she thought would allow us to get inside."

"So said the spider to the fly," murmured Greg, gazing nervously at the now wide open hatch. A brightly lighted corridor could be seen on the other side.

"You must like that saying," Jason responded, with a nervous laugh. He remembered Greg saying the same thing when they had originally been exploring the wreck on the Moon. "Well, let's see what we can find." With that, Jason stepped through the hatch with the others following close behind.

They found themselves in a small, short corridor with closed hatches on both ends. All the lights were on, and the corridor looked as if it had been built yesterday. Everything looked new and clean.

"This doesn't look like an old base built nearly 100 years ago," Greg stated. "There's no dust and no signs of wear. Which way?"

"Let's try that hatch first," replied Jason, pointing toward the nearest. Going to the hatch, he opened it and found it was actually a large air lock.

Everyone crowded inside, and once the hatch was shut, a series of different colored lights began coming on. Each light stayed on for about twenty seconds and then another series of colored lights would come on.

"What's going on?" Karl Stern asked, confused.

"Decontamination," replied Doctor Andrea Oleson, gazing speculatively at the lights. "I would guess we are being bombarded with specific radiation frequencies aimed at destroying microorganisms."

"Are they safe?" Greg asked. He still wanted to have some more kids some day.

"Should be," Andrea replied.

"I don't understand," said Lisa, sounding confused. "If they had this type of decontamination procedure 100 years ago, why didn't it work against the flu?"

"This might be something they instituted afterwards," Andrea responded.

Doctor Oleson wished she knew what the frequencies were. This was medical science considerably ahead of anything Earth was capable of. This type of decontamination could be of great use in hospitals and other areas where the threat of contagious diseases being spread existed.

The lights suddenly returned to normal, and a light liquid spray began spraying from the walls, floor, and ceiling. This continued for a full minute and then the room began heating up.

"More decontamination," Andrea explained with a satisfied nod. "Commander, I don't believe this is being done by a computer. There has to be someone in charge. There has to be a reason why we are being subjected to these decontamination procedures."

"It could be the AI on the Vindication," responded Lisa, turning to face Andrea. "She is very similar to Ariel, and this could now be part of her programming in order to keep the base safe."

"But why, if there are no survivors from the evacuation fleet?" Andrea countered. Then, turning to face Jason, she continued. "No Commander, this isn't a computer. I think we need to be prepared to meet survivors very shortly. Perhaps on the other side of that door!"

Jason looked around the group. He felt that Doctor Oleson might be correct. "If we do encounter someone, don't make any sudden moves. I will do the talking."

A noise attracted Jason's attention and, turning around, he saw the hatch opposite the one they had just come through start to open. The hatch swung slowly open, and Jason gestured for the others to follow him. Stepping cautiously through he came to a sudden stop, letting out a sharp breath and slowly raised his hands in a non-threatening gesture. The others behind him did the same thing.

Standing in front of Jason were six heavily armed men, all in dark blue military uniforms. All six had their weapons leveled at Jason and the people with him. From the looks on their faces, they were prepared to use them if necessary.

"We mean no harm," Jason spoke over his suit's com system, hoping these people could understand him. Doctor Oleson had been right. There were survivors!

One of the men stepped forward and gazed speculatively at Jason. He raised a small communication device to his mouth and spoke into it, never taking his eyes off of Jason.

"Commander Strong, you will follow Captain Simms to our detention area until we decide what to do with you," a female voice spoke over the suit's com system.

"Clarissa?" asked Jason wondering if the female voice was the AI on the Vindication.

"That's correct, Commander Strong. We have been monitoring you for quite some time. You will not be harmed, but we need to awaken some people who are more qualified to deal with this situation."

"Can you contact Ariel and let her know we're okay?" Jason asked.

He knew the AI and Colonel Greene would be extremely worried since communication had been lost so abruptly. Ariel might believe the shuttle had been destroyed by the base's defensive systems. If they were reported missing, he didn't want to think about what his sister and Greg's wife would feel like. It would be devastating to them.

"Perhaps later," Clarissa replied noncommittally. "That is not my decision to make. The admiral will have to decide that. Now please follow Captain Simms."

"Better do as she asks," Lisa suggested. She had been following the conversation over her suit com system. She was thrilled to learn that the other AI had survived. "Clarissa said we wouldn't be harmed."

They followed Captain Simms through a series of brightly lit corridors until they arrived at a large room with a number of chairs, a few tables, and some bunks against one wall. There was another door on the far end.

"You will remain here until the admiral is ready to see you," Clarissa informed them. "Once Captain Simms and his marines have left, you may remove your suits. You will find suitable clothing to wear through the door at the far end of the room. This facility is quite secure, and there is no way for you to leave without the door being opened from the outside."

"Are we prisoners?" asked Jason, wanting to know what their status was. At least they hadn't been separated.

"No, you're not prisoners," Clarissa responded. "It is just prudent that we take appropriate safety precautions while certain tests are run."

"You're worried about diseases," Andrea said in sudden realization. "After what happened with the Spanish Flu, you're not taking any chances."

"That's correct, Doctor Oleson," Clarissa replied. "We may be requesting your expertise in this matter later. We believe our decontamination procedures are now effective against contagions such as your flu. We would like to make sure."

Captain Simms and his marines left, and Jason found that they were alone for the time being. "Let's get these suits off. We may be here for awhile."

"Jason, do you know what this means?" Lisa said with excitement in her voice. "This base is fully active and has Federation survivors in it. We can learn so much from them."

"They could teach us their science and manufacturing techniques," Adam said with a nod. He had so many questions he would like to ask. "We could move forward a hundred years in the next decade with their help."

"If they're willing to help us," Greg said, shaking his head in doubt. "And if they are willing to help, why have they stayed hidden all of these years?"

Everyone stared at Greg, wondering about what he had just said. There was a mystery here; one that needed to be solved. They had found the base and, more importantly, had found survivors from the Human Federation of Worlds.

"They seem to know an awful lot about us," Jason said, turning to face Lisa. "How can that be?"

"I don't know," replied Lisa shaking her head. "Obviously they have been listening to our communications, but how did Clarissa know that Andrea is a doctor?"

"From what Clarissa said they evidently found a cure for the Spanish Flu," Andrea added, her eyes taking on a thoughtful look. "Depending on when they found the cure, there could have been more survivors than we originally thought."

"Let's get out of these suits and change clothes," suggested Jason, walking toward the door at the far end of the room. "We won't know what's going on until we talk to this admiral of theirs."

Jason also wondered about Lieutenant Addison and Professor Tennyson, who were still back in the shuttle. He had a suspicion the two would be joining them shortly. There were a lot of questions he would like to have answered.

Chapter Three

It was less than two hours later when a nervous looking Lieutenant Addison and Marvin Tennyson were brought in by the marines. The marines said nothing, just left the two and departed, locking the door behind them.

"Tough looking group," muttered Greg, staring at the closed door.

He didn't like having an assault rifle pointed at him. It still felt as if they were being held prisoners. Those marines were clearly not to be messed with.

"Commander Strong," Addison spoke with relief in his voice at seeing everyone else was okay. "Those marines came into the landing bay. A female voice came over the com system ordering us to leave the shuttle and go with the marines. I didn't think we should resist."

"You did the correct thing, Lieutenant," Jason responded with a nod. He was relieved there hadn't been an incident. "The people on this base are in charge now, we just have to wait and see what happens."

"But who are they?" asked Greg, walking over to stand next to Jason. He had searched the room very thoroughly. There was no way out except through the door they had come in through. "They don't seem very friendly."

"Obviously survivors from the Federation evacuation fleet," commented Doctor Oleson, looking thoughtful. "They seemed to be well organized and were waiting for us. It wouldn't surprise me if there are a lot more."

"That was Clarissa that spoke to us," Lisa added, still excited to find that the other AI had survived. "She is as intelligent as Ariel and just as capable."

"If Clarissa survived, that means the Vindication is here somewhere," added Jason, looking meaningfully at Greg.

"Did you get a close look at those assault rifles their marines were carrying?" continued Greg, folding his arms across his chest. Those marines hadn't acted very friendly, and that worried him. "We don't have anything similar that I am aware of. Those weapons were designed to do some major damage at close range."

"They obviously have a security force of well trained marines," Jason responded. He looked over at Greg. "They have acted very professional, which shows a high level of training."

Greg nodded his head in agreement, realizing Jason was correct. He knew those marines had only been doing their job. "A major part of their military must have survived. I wonder just how many of their warships are inside this asteroid."

They were interrupted as the door to their holding area opened and a man and a woman entered. The man was wearing a dark blue military uniform, and the woman was dressed in a colorful blouse and pants. The man was of average height with brown hair and obviously spent a lot of time working out. The woman was a brunette and very striking.

"Hello, I am Keela Ryson the chief medical officer for this facility," the woman spoke in a friendly voice. Then, indicating the officer, she continued. "This is Colonel Runess, our Chief of Security."

"We're pleased to meet you," Jason said, his eyes sweeping over the two. He noticed quickly that neither of the two were armed.

"How come you're not wearing some type of protective suits?" asked Andrea, stepping up next to Jason. "Are you not worried about possible diseases we may be carrying?"

Keela's eyes focused on Doctor Oleson, and then she smiled. "No, we're not anymore. At least not here in the base. Everyone in the base has been inoculated against Earth diseases; we have been for a number of years now. We have also been analyzing the air inside this holding facility to detect any airborne pathogens that you might be carrying. We have found nothing that could be considered dangerous."

"Then why all the precautions?" asked Jason, recalling all the decontamination procedures they had gone through in the airlock.

"Just standard precautions, now," Keela replied. "I am sure Doctor Oleson understands. We also want to make sure there are no new microorganisms in your systems that we're not protected against. Several nurses will be in shortly to take blood samples from each of you to confirm that. They will also be inoculating all of you against diseases we may have that you would have no immunity against. I can assure you we have nothing close to your flu. Colonel Runess and I will go through decontamination immediately upon leaving here as a precaution, even though I suspect it isn't actually necessary."

"How long will we have to be in isolation?" Andrea asked, curiously. "I assume we will have to stay here until all the tests have been run."

"About 72 hours," Keela replied with a friendly nod. "That will give time for the inoculations to take effect. Perhaps by then the admiral will be ready to see you."

"Who is this admiral we keep hearing mentioned?" Jason asked. "Even Clarissa mentioned him."

"Admiral Hedon Streth the founder of this base," Colonel Runess answered in an even voice.

"The founder of the base," Greg broke in, his eyes growing wide in confusion. "That was nearly 100 years ago! How is that possible?"

"That's correct, Mister Johnson," Keela replied with a mysterious smile. "He has been in cryosleep for much of that time. This will only be the fourth time we have awakened him."

"Cryosleep?" repeated Doctor Oleson, looking confused. "Is that some type of suspended animation?"

Keela laughed and nodded her head. "In a way. We have learned how to lower the body temperature to greatly slow the aging process."

"The admiral is very important to us," Colonel Runess added. "If not for him, none of us would be here."

"Can we get a message out to Ariel to let her know we're okay?" Jason asked. "Our people back on the Moon will be worried about us."

He didn't want their families to be upset. He knew how his sister and Greg's wife would react if they heard contact had been lost with the shuttle. He remembered how they had reacted when contact had been lost with the New Beginnings mission.

"That is being arranged," Colonel Runess replied with a slight nod of his head. "Clarissa will send a message to Ariel reporting that you all are okay as soon as the admiral approves it. She will use an encrypted Federation code that your military will not be able to break if it is intercepted. There will also be some very explicit instructions for Ariel. We don't want word of this base to get out. I believe your Colonel Greene will understand."

"You seem to know a lot about our people," Lisa said, looking at Colonel Runess and feeling perplexed. "How is that possible?"

"We have some spy satellites in orbit around both the Earth and the Moon," Colonel Runess answered, shifting his gaze to Lisa. "We also have a direct line to Ariel that she is not aware of. Everything she has done and found out about all of you since the Avenger was discovered has been transmitted on a secure line to our base."

Jason nodded. He had suspected something like this for awhile now. It was the only explanation for some of the things these people seemed to know. It was a surprise to realize that these people had been watching the Earth and the Moon both. Jason wondered how long this clandestine surveillance had been going on.

"These satellites must be made of some type of stealth material or we would have detected them by now," Lieutenant Addison commented. He knew a little about stealth technology from his training in the air force.

"That's correct, Lieutenant," replied Runess, nodding his head. "We thought it best that your world not know of our existence. Now that may have to change."

"I will call my nurses in. They can draw the blood samples as well as inoculate you against our diseases," Keela spoke. "Then, in a few days, we can let you out of here and answer some more of your questions. For the time being, I would suggest that you take it easy and rest. You may feel some slight nausea from the inoculations, but it shouldn't be anything serious."

"One more thing," added Colonel Runess, looking thoughtfully at Jason. "Ariel has named you commander of the Avenger. That's a very positive development as far as we're concerned. She would not have named you her commander if you weren't qualified. I will mention that to the admiral when he awakens."

Colonel Runess and Keela left, and two nurses entered the room. They were carrying the instruments needed to draw blood as well as to give the inoculations.

"Damn," Greg muttered. He didn't like needles.

One of the nurses smiled and indicated for Greg to roll up his sleeve. She was holding what looked like some type of automated syringe. Why do I always have to be first, Greg wondered?

The next day on board the Avenger, Ariel was surprised when a message from the direction of Ceres was received by one of her repaired communication devices. She was elated when she realized the message was from Clarissa. For a moment, Ariel felt immense relief at not being so alone. Clarissa had survived! After receiving the message and the orders it contained, she sent for Colonel Greene.

Colonel Greene arrived in the Command Center and was surprised to see that no one was inside. He had strict standing orders that at least two people were to be in the Command Center at all times. Looking at the main viewscreen, he saw Ariel staring at him with a mysterious smile. What's going on, he wondered?

"Why is no one on duty in the Command Center, Ariel?"

"I sent them away, Colonel Greene."

"On whose authority," he asked confused. This was unlike Ariel. She had been extremely cooperative recently. She also enjoyed having people in the Command Center.

"I have received new orders from Ceres which I must obey."

"Ceres!" exclaimed Colonel Greene, his eyes widening. They had lost contact with Commander Strong the day before. Had they managed to reestablish communication?

"Was it Commander Strong?"

"No, sir, my orders come from a higher authority."

Colonel Greene felt a chill run through him. "Who?"

"The orders originated from the Federation base inside Ceres and were sent by Clarissa, the AI of the light cruiser Vindication. The orders must be obeyed unless countered by the commander of First Fleet."

"First Fleet?" Colonel Greene asked confused. What was happening on that asteroid? "I don't understand."

"First Fleet is comprised of the warships that escorted the civilian ships to this solar system. They are all that remains of the Federation space forces. The fleet is under the command of Fleet Admiral Hedon Streth."

"This admiral is still alive?" asked Colonel Greene, feeling uneasy. He suddenly realized that the humans on the Avenger were no longer in charge. What did all of this mean?

"Yes, he is. He has been awakened to handle the situation with our shuttle and Commander Strong. Commander Strong's people are inside the base and are all safe. There can be no word of this conversation to anyone, Colonel Greene. All you are allowed to say is that contact has been reestablished with Commander Strong and the mission is continuing. We will be contacted later with additional updates and orders."

Colonel Greene sat down in the commander's chair behind the center console. He could feel his heart pounding in his chest. The Federation base on Ceres was intact and obviously operational. He let out a long breath and gazed at Ariel. The young woman on the screen was silent and looked serene, almost happy. She's back in her Federation again, Colonel Greene realized. He wondered what all of this would mean. For nearly an hour, Colonel Greene sat thinking about the ramifications of what Ariel had told him. His world was about to change again. The Hocklyns were in the future, and there was no doubt that this base on Ceres and this admiral would play a huge role in what was to come.

The 72 hours passed rapidly, and Colonel Runess and Keela returned to the detention area. They called the detainees together to let them know the results of their medical tests.

"According to our tests it is safe for all of you to leave this room," Keela began with a smile, knowing how hard it must have been for all eight of these people to be left in detention with so many unanswered questions.

"The first thing we want to do is give all of you a tour of the base," Colonel Runess explained. "Once you have realized what we have accomplished here, you will meet with Admiral Streth for a debriefing."

"We will divide you into two groups," Keela continued. "Professor Stern, Doctor Oleson, Professor Tennyson, and Mister Simmins will come with me. The rest of you will be going with Colonel Runess."

"What are we going to see?" Greg asked, thrilled at the prospect of finally getting out of this room. He had spent nearly four weeks in several small rooms on the Avenger, and this had reminded him of that.

Colonel Runess smiled slightly looking at Greg. "I have been told to take you to the light cruiser Vindication. I would think you would like to see what an intact Federation warship looks like."

Greg's eyes widened. This was like a dream come true. "Let's go!"

They made their way through numerous corridors, and as they went deeper into the base, they started to see more people. Many were dressed in military uniforms, but quite a few were obviously civilians. Some doors were open, and they could see people working. They were operating equipment and doing other jobs, which mystified the group. Most of the equipment they were operating was unlike anything on

Earth. In some of the more sensitive areas, marine guards were posted and they were not allowed entrance.

"Once you have spoken to Admiral Streth you may be allowed into some of those departments," Colonel Runess commented when asked about what was being guarded. "Even here on Ceres we have secrets that need to be protected."

"What happened after your fleet became infected with the flu?" Jason asked, curiously. "We know it had spread to some of the civilian ships."

Colonel Runess was silent for a moment. He hadn't been alive at the time, but his parents had told him about the horrors and hardships many families had faced.

"It was a bad time for everyone," he said with a sad forlorn look upon his face. "The civilians thought they had found a new home, one that was safe from the Hocklyns where they could start over and raise their families. Earth was so much like our home planets."

"But some of your people became infected with the Spanish Flu while they were down on Earth and brought it back up to the civilian fleet," spoke Jason, recalling what Ariel had told them.

"Yes, we had no immunity to this flu virus," Colonel Runess answered with a far away look in his eyes. "We had diseases on our home planets, but nothing like your flu. Hundreds became sick and then started to die. The disease spread rapidly. The admiral ordered all the sick to be quarantined on four civilian vessels in an attempt to halt the spread of the disease. In the end it took six ships, and we lost thousands."

Everyone had stopped walking and were listening raptly to the colonel. "Thousands," Lisa repeated in a poignant voice.

She could imagine the horror. Families being split apart in an effort to stop the disease. Husbands, wives, and children becoming infected and having to be taken away from those they loved. It would have been a nightmare.

"In the end, we lost 18,000 of the 40,000 civilians that were part of the fleet," Colonel Runess said in a somber voice. "When we reached Ceres, there were nearly 300 suicides from family members who had lost nearly everyone. It was a very bad time for the fleet."

"But you managed to survive," Jason commented. He didn't know what he would have done if faced with the same situation the Federation survivors had found themselves in. "You overcame the disease and managed to build this base."

"Yes, but it was a very difficult and trying time for everyone. The docking bays are just down this corridor," continued Colonel Runess, trying to sound more lighthearted. The Spanish Flu and the deaths were ancient history, a history he wished he could forget. However, it was a crucial part of what had helped to create the Ceres base.

They continued on down the corridor and passed through a large double airlock. Stepping through, they found themselves in a brightly lit, cavernous bay. There were two ships in the bay; both of the light cruiser class.

"My God, they're huge!" Greg cried in admiration, gazing at the warships. He had expected them to be large, but the reality of what he was seeing still astonished him.

There were two light cruisers in the bay. Each one was 600 meters in length and completely undamaged. Numerous people, as well as work robots, were visible going about their jobs. The work robots did indeed look like giant spiders.

"Are they space worthy?" Greg asked with his eyes focused on the ships. "I mean, could you fly them to another star today if you wanted to?"

"Yes," Colonel Runess replied with a nod. "We keep all of our warships at a state of readiness. We don't expect to see the Hocklyns for 268 years, but there is always the possibility that one of their long-range scouts could find us."

"How likely?" Jason asked with narrowed eyes. If the Hocklyns were to find Earth now, it would be a disaster. It would be years before Earth would be capable of putting up any kind of defense against the advanced weapons of the Hocklyns.

"Not very," replied Colonel Runess, noticing Jason's concern. "But we prefer not to take any chances. We have taken some steps to make sure Earth isn't found. The admiral will explain those to you later."

"How many warships do you have in the base?" asked Greg, his eyes still focused on the cruisers.

He wondered how many bays like this were inside Ceres. On one of the ships, several of the hatches were open and the railgun turrets were visible. From this position, the weapons looked deadly and ready to take on an enemy.

"Admiral Streth will have to give you that information," Colonel Runess replied civilly "Some of that information is classified."

Jason nodded. "These ships are impressive, Colonel. I just hope Earth can build something like them one of these days."

"Let's go inside the Vindication. I believe that Clarissa wants to speak with your group."

They made their way down several ramps and finally came to a boarding ramp that led inside the cruiser. They passed several work robots on the way, as well as other people going about their jobs. They acted as if visitors from Earth were a common occurrence.

They entered the cruiser, and after awhile they started to feel more at home as the corridors became more familiar as they neared the Command Center. They found the hatch to the Command Center to be open, but two heavily armed marines were standing outside in the corridor.

Stepping inside the Command Center, Jason was surprised to see that it was fully manned. "Do you always keep full crews on your ships while they are docked inside Ceres?" asked Jason, turning to look at Colonel Runess.

"We only have partial crews on the ships," Colonel Runess responded. "At any one time only about ten percent of a ship's crew is on board. If there is an emergency, the ship can be ready to launch by the time the rest of the crew is recalled. That's one reason why the Command Center is always manned."

"Hello," a young feminine voice spoke from the front of the Command Center.

Turning to face the voice, Jason saw Clarissa. Clarissa was a pretty blonde with deep blue eyes and a friendly face. "Hello Clarissa," Jason responded, his eyes drawn to the AI.

"All these AIs are gorgeous," muttered Greg, shaking his head and looking at Clarissa. The Federation obviously had a good taste in women.

"Thank you, Mister Johnson," Clarissa replied with a wide smile.

Greg felt his face flush. He had forgotten how well the AIs could hear in the Command Center.

"I believe you have some questions for me, Commander Strong," Clarissa stated, her eyes focusing on Jason.

For the next hour, they all talked. Jason asked several questions, and Clarissa in return asked numerous questions about Ariel. One of the things that Jason and Lisa discovered was that the Federation survivors hadn't known at first that Ariel had survived. It was only after Jason and Greg had flown their lander over the Avenger, causing the emergency beacon to activate, that Ariel had used enough power for Clarissa to detect the AI's presence on the wrecked ship. It had been decided not to contact Ariel in the beginning, but to wait and see what happened with the visitors from Earth.

Jason was surprised how much alike the two AIs were, but they were also very different. Lisa had dozens of technical questions she was plying Clarissa with. Some Clarissa answered, and others she put off.

"You will need to consult the admiral," she would say.

Jason was curious about this Admiral Streth. These people obviously had a lot of respect for him, almost reverence. He knew he would be meeting him soon and perhaps then more of his questions would be answered.

"Would you like to see Engineering?" Colonel Runess asked. He knew that the Engineering section on the Avenger had been destroyed.

"That would be great," Jason answered. He wanted to see what the rest of the Avenger would have looked like if it were still intact. "On the Avenger, everything behind the flight bay is destroyed, missing, or scattered in the crater."

"That's what I have been told," Colonel Runess replied with a sad look in his eyes. "It's surprising that Ariel survived as badly damaged as the Avenger is."

Sometime later, they were in Engineering, looking in awe at the technology that had allowed the Human Federation of Worlds to spread across the stars. The chief engineer had patiently explained to the group, in simple terms, how the FTL core worked as well as the ship's powerful sublight drive.

"This is all amazing," Lieutenant Addison spoke, his eyes trying to take everything in.

He had asked the chief engineer some questions but had realized quickly that he didn't have the necessary technological knowledge to understand what the man was trying to explain. In the background, he could hear a faint hum from the Vindication's two high-energy fusion reactors.

Jason gazed at all the consoles and controls, in front of which a few of the ship's Engineering crew were busy monitoring the ship's functions. He began to realize just what would be involved in order to build a warship such as this. With a sinking feeling, he knew that it would be decades before Earth was ready for this advanced technology. If introduced too quickly, it would disrupt the planet's economy and who knows what else. Something else would have to be done. Jason had a vague idea forming in the back of his mind, but he would have to discuss it with Colonel Greene when they returned to the Moon.

Colonel Runess led them from the Vindication and around more of the base. The base was immense. Jason continued to marvel at all the work that had been done. There were more people about as they went deeper into the base, as well as more of the eight legged work robots.

"What all can these work robots do?" asked Lieutenant Addison, stopping to examine one a little closer.

The robot had eight tentacles attached to an oval shaped body. A small metal globe rested on top. This was obliviously the computer that controlled the robot.

"You would be surprised," Colonel Runess answered with a smile. "They can be programmed to do almost anything. They can work about sixteen hours before they need to return to their charging stations. We have nearly a thousand of these currently in the base involved in various projects. They are monitored from a central station by some of our engineers and the base's main computer."

"Do these robots do all the construction going on in the base?" Greg asked curiously.

He could see the benefits of using the robots. They wouldn't get tired, and their work would be constant. The robots also could do the more dangerous jobs so a human life wouldn't be placed in jeopardy. They wouldn't need to stop for breaks or to eat lunch either. These would be highly useful down on Earth in some of the construction jobs as well as other jobs that were deemed unsafe.

"No," Colonel Runess responded, his eyes shifting to Greg. "Most of the time they work side by side with base personnel. It's something we're used to. They're capable of doing very technical work if programmed properly."

As they continued their tour, Colonel Runess showed them automated factories, parts storage bays, numerous weapons production and storage areas, power plants, and even where one of the colony ships was berthed.

They were standing on a large metal balcony overlooking a cavernous bay. Jason looked at the colony ship in awe; it was massive! Jason knew it was nearly 2,000 meters in length. The ship dominated the bay, and he could see numerous work robots constantly going in and out of the open hatches.

"What are the work robots doing?" Jason asked curiously. They seemed to be getting the ship ready for something.

"The admiral will explain that," replied Colonel Runess, glancing down at the timepiece on his wrist and seeing it was almost time to see the admiral. "But first I have one more thing I need to show you."

Colonel Runess led them to another corridor and opened a sealed hatch. On the other side was what looked like an Earth subway system. The colonel indicated for them to get inside a waiting vehicle that was setting in the tunnel. They all entered and sat down in the large, comfortable seats. The vehicle began to move, and they were soon going down the lighted tunnel at a high speed.

"We're going about twenty-five kilometers inside of Ceres," Colonel Runess explained.

Jason and Greg looked at each other. At the speed the vehicle they were in was traveling, that wouldn't take long. The walls of the tunnel almost seemed to be a blur.

After a few minutes, the vehicle slowed and then came to a stop at a large platform where there were other transit vehicles. Four heavily armed marines stood on the platform. There were other people there as well that had gotten out of other transit vehicles. Most seemed to be civilians with a few military personnel mixed in. Jason and his people got out of the vehicle and Colonel Runess led them through a large open hatch. They went down a wide corridor full of people and then through a large double airlock. Four more marine guards watched the new arrivals as they stepped outside the open airlock.

"There sure is a lot of security in this area," Greg commented. Looking forward, he noticed four large open hatches. The light coming through them seemed more like regular sunlight.

The group walked over, stepped through one of the open hatches, and then came to a sudden stop, their eyes growing wide in disbelief at what they were seeing. It was as if they had entered another world. They were in a massive cavern that stretched for nearly as far as the eye could see. In the center of the cavern was a modern city surrounded by rolling hills, grassland, and cultivated soil. There were even some small rivers and several lakes visible.

"This is where we live," Colonel Runess explained with satisfaction in his voice. "In case of an emergency, the hatch at the transit station can be sealed. The airlocks shut, and the four large hatches behind us can be sealed off also. We keep a full squad of marines in that area at all times as a precaution."

"It's beautiful," Lisa spoke, her eyes trying to take everything in. "It must have taken you years to build this and get the ecosystem all worked out."

"Twenty-two years," replied Colonel Runess, nodding his head. "It reminds us of home and gives our people a sense of normalcy. The Hocklyns took everything away from us, but here we have managed to rebuild."

"How many people are here on Ceres?" Jason asked, not sure if Colonel Runess would give out that information.

"Our last census indicated we had 122,000 people currently on Ceres," Colonel Runess answered. "Our habitable area here is thirty kilometers long and twenty kilometers wide. There is already talk about building a second, larger habitat farther inside the asteroid."

They stood for several minutes gazing out across the park-like view, astonished at what the Federation survivors had managed to build. To Jason, this was more amazing than the ships they had seen.

"I think it's time you meet our admiral," Colonel Runess spoke. "He is highly interested in meeting you."

-

Colonel Runess led them down an adjacent corridor and, after walking for a few minutes, they came to a heavily guarded door. Four marines with body armor and heavy assault rifles stood guard outside the entrance. For the first time, Colonel Runess had to show his identification before the group was allowed to enter. Once inside, they found themselves standing in a lobby with two female fleet personnel sitting behind a large desk.

"Admiral Streth will see you now," one of them spoke, indicating a door behind them. "The rest of your group is already inside."

Taking a deep breath, Jason followed Colonel Runess inside the indicated door. Perhaps finally he would get some of the answers he had been searching for.

-

Admiral Streth watched the new arrivals with interest. He was seated behind a large desk and had been waiting for the Earth human's commander to arrive. This was only the fourth time he had been awakened since he had entered cryosleep. He also knew this might very well be the most important one. The man in front of him was obviously one used to giving orders. He stood unafraid in front of the admiral but had a very curious look upon his face. This was a human from Earth, as were the rest of the group that had come with him. Something the admiral had been waiting on for nearly 100 years.

"I am Admiral Streth, commander of this base and of First Fleet," Hedon spoke, standing up and extending his hand.

Jason grasped the admiral's hand and shook it. "I am Commander Jason Strong of Earth. We have come a long way to meet you, sir."

Admiral Streth smiled and indicated for everyone to sit down. "I know you have a lot of questions, probably the first being why we have never contacted Earth."

"That would be my first question," Jason confirmed with a nod. "You obviously have the ability to do so."

"We were waiting for your world to reach the point where it could handle our advanced technology. We did not want to create a culture shock and cause your world and society to fall into chaos. Your arrival here indicates that it is time for us to contact the leaders of your world and set certain plans into motion."

"We know about the Hocklyns and what happened to the Human Federation of Worlds," Jason said. "We have learned a lot from Ariel."

"Then you know of the threat that is coming our way in another 268 or so of your years."

"Yes, Admiral," Jason responded. "We know we will have to fight."

"I haven't had a chance to speak in detail with my people about what all Ariel has told you," Admiral Streth said, his eyes turning thoughtful. "Even during the war, Ariel was very useful. In hindsight, we should have put more of the AIs on our ships. I was glad to hear that she survived."

"Ariel is a good friend," Jason spoke with a nod.

"That's good," Admiral Streth replied, pleased with the answer. "We will join together in this. The Hocklyns will not be allowed to destroy another human world."

"Did you fight the Hocklyns?" Greg asked in a subdued voice. "Were you involved in the battles?"

"Yes," Admiral Streth replied his eyes shifting over to Greg. "I was involved in several engagements against them. They are very powerful, and their ships are extremely difficult to destroy."

"That's why you have been in cryosleep," Jason said with dawning realization. "We will need your experience when we face the Hocklyns."

Admiral Streth gazed at Jason for a long moment. "Yes, Commander. There are a number of us that are waiting in cryosleep. It is hoped that our experience will give us the edge we need to stop the Hocklyns this time."

For the next several hours, the group talked with Admiral Streth. They asked numerous questions, most of which the admiral was willing to answer. A few he refrained from, saying that particular question would have to wait for a later time. He spoke about the war with the Hocklyns, what had transpired, and why. He also spoke in depth about his plans for the future and the role he hoped Earth would be willing to play.

"It will take all of us working together if we want to survive this," he said finally. "When you return to Earth, I will be sending another shuttle with you. It is considerably larger than the one you arrived on. There will be a liaison from this base going along to speak with your governments. I am also sending some technicians and work robots to help repair the surviving sections of the Avenger. For now, it will serve as a secure meeting place for us as well as a possible future training center. At some point in time, we will be sending an additional power source. The small fusion reactor Ariel is currently using was not designed to function as the main power supply for the ship. We will send something more appropriate and will show your people how to install it."

Jason nodded, this meeting had gone much better than he had expected. He had learned so much, but there was still so much more. "We saw the colony ship in its bay. It looks as if it's being prepared for launch."

"Yes, it is," Admiral Streth replied with a nod. "It's going on a resupply mission."

"Where to?" asked Jason, feeling curious about where the ship could be going. Did the admiral's people have other bases in the Solar System?

"I have a special surprise for you and Mr. Johnson. There is a shuttle leaving in a few hours that will rendezvous with a light cruiser on picket duty near your system's cometary ring. If the two of you would like to go, there is something else I would like you to see. You will be gone for about six days, but I promise you, it will be worth it. It is also where the colony ship will be going in a few more days."

Jason nodded, not sure what to say. To get to travel on one of the Federation's warships was something he couldn't turn down. He knew without looking that Greg was thinking the same thing.

Jason and Greg sat in the shuttle, excited about the prospect of getting to go aboard an actual Federation light cruiser for six days. Admiral Streth had been silent about where they were going, but Jason had the impression their eventual destination was not in Earth's Solar System. Across from Jason and Greg sat Admiral Streth. They had been surprised to find out that he was going along with them. The shuttle had made a micro-jump as soon as it had cleared the gravity well of Ceres. Both had been a little pale from the queasiness the jump had caused.

"I haven't been outside of the Solar System in over 100 years," spoke Admiral Streth, looking over at the two Earth humans. "I believe the two of you will enjoy this experience."

Outside the shuttle, two space fighters flew in formation, keeping a protective eye on the shuttle. The fighters had come from the light cruiser they were approaching. On board the cruiser, the commander was keeping a close watch on the shuttle. The admiral was on board, and his safety was paramount.

The shuttle made its approach to the cruiser and slid easily into the brightly lighted flight bay. The pilot landed the shuttle without the faintest hint of a jar. This brought a smile to the admiral's face. It was good to see the members of the fleet were still well trained.

Admiral Streth turned to Jason and Greg. "We will proceed to the Command Center. I am sure both of you would like to see a light cruiser in full operation. We will be making an FTL jump to our destination. Matter of fact, there will be three jumps."

"Where are we going?" Jason asked curiously as all three stood up and moved toward the hatch, which was now opening. Admiral Streth had just confirmed that they would be leaving the Solar System.

"To a star system 27 light years core-ward from Earth," Admiral Streth replied with an enigmatic smile. "There is a surprise there I want the two of you to see."

Stepping outside the hatch, the admiral was surprised and pleased to see a full platoon of marines in their parade dress uniforms standing at attention. The commander of the ship was also present, as well as several other of the ship's officers.

"Admiral of the fleet arriving!" a voice boomed as the admiral descended the ramp.

Jason and Greg gazed at this obvious showing of respect and reverence for the admiral. The man was truly loved by the men and women under his command, even after all of this time.

"Commander Andrew Benson reporting, sir!" the commander of the ship spoke, saluting the admiral.

"At ease Commander," replied Admiral Streth, saluting the commander and then turning to salute the assembled marines. "You have an excellent looking group here, Commander."

"Thank you, sir," Commander Benson replied. "If you will follow me, we will go to the Command Center. We're ready to jump on your order."

The group made their way through the ship with a small escort of marines. Upon reaching the Command Center, they were allowed admittance and soon were standing around the holographic plotting table.

"Course is set for New Tellus, sir," the Navigation officer reported.

"Very well, you may jump at your discretion," Admiral Streth replied. It felt good to be in the Command Center of a warship again. It almost felt like the old days.

"We will arrive in the New Tellus System in twenty hours," Commander Benson informed Admiral Streth.

Jason and Greg just looked at each other. They could barely believe what they had just heard. They were traveling to another solar system 27 light years away.

Admiral Streth turned toward the two with an all knowing smile. "After each jump the ship's engineers will fine tune the FTL drive and allow the core to cool down. This is a safety procedure to ensure that we don't jump too close to a planet or a moon's gravity well. If we were to do so, it could seriously damage the drive. In an emergency, we can make another jump almost immediately with relative safety."

"We also try to limit our jumps to about five light years," Commander Benson added. "The drives are capable of more, but we try not to overtax the system."

Jason nodded. It was becoming more evident every minute just how far Earth would have to advance before it was ready for this type of advanced technology. It was amazing the difference a fully trained crew made in the Command Center. Normally, on the Avenger, only a few people were present and they were usually asking Ariel questions. Ariel was currently controlling all the systems on the Avenger.

"If you gentlemen will observe the main viewscreen you will see the warp vortex form," Commander Benson said, gesturing toward the large screen on the front wall of the Command Center.

As Jason and Greg watched, a blue-white vortex formed in front of the cruiser. A moment later, the vortex seemed to grow rapidly as the cruiser flew into it. Jason felt a wrenching feeling in his gut, and then everything returned to normal.

"Glad I didn't eat a big meal," Greg commented with a pale face.

"Takes some getting used to," Admiral Streth remarked with a knowing smile. "I lost my meal the first time I experienced a jump."

Jason looked around the bustling Command Center. Everyone seemed to be busy working at their consoles and talking to different sections of the ship over the com system. It was evident that this was a well trained and knowledgeable crew.

The next day, the cruiser exited another blue-white vortex into the New Tellus System. For four more hours, the ship cruised on its sublight drive and finally rendezvoused with another ship.

Admiral Streth gazed at the viewscreen, felt his heart racing, and knew his breathing had picked up. A truly massive warship was on the viewscreen. It was the flagship of First Fleet and his personal command. The battle cruiser StarStrike was waiting for him.

"What is that?" Greg spoke, his eyes growing wide. If that ship was as large as it looked on the viewscreen, it was much larger than a light cruiser. This had to be one of the Federation's first line warships. He had wondered if any had survived.

"That, my friends, is the StarStrike," Admiral Streth replied with a fond smile. "She is a Conqueror Class Command Battle Cruiser. The StarStrike is 1,200 meters long and 250 meters wide. She is the most powerful ship in the fleet."

Greg took a step back. His eyes were open wide, and his heart was racing. Jason and he had thought a light cruiser was impressive. Nothing they had seen thus far could compare to what was showing on the viewscreen in front of them.

"Is this your largest warship?" Greg asked, intrigued. He couldn't imagine anything bigger.

"No," replied Admiral Streth shaking his head. "A battle carrier is bigger, but it's not as heavily armed as the StarStrike. We currently don't have a battle carrier deployed."

"But you do have one?" pressed Greg, wanting to see one.

"There are two in their bays on Ceres," Admiral Streth responded. "When we get back I will take you and Commander Strong on a personal tour. The battle carriers carry our air wings."

Several hours later, they were in the Command Center of the StarStrike. Jason gazed in amazement at everything around him. Consoles, viewscreens, situation boards, and control stations were all about him and manned by a confident group of men and women. The ship gave off a feeling of ultimate power. But a shadow of worry hung in the back of Jason's mind. If the Federation had lost the war against the Hocklyns with ships like the StarStrike, what was going to happen in 268 more years? Could the Hocklyns even be stopped? Jason was beginning to have his doubts. The Hocklyns might be an unstoppable force.

Since boarding the StarStrike, they had micro-jumped closer to New Tellus and were now approaching the planet on the ship's powerful sublight drive. Jason knew that two light cruisers were escorting the flagship in toward the planet. Glancing down at the holographic plotting table, it also showed six space fighters flying CAP around the three warships.

As they neared the blue-white globe that was steadily growing on the viewscreen, Admiral Streth turned toward Jason and Greg. "We have a small settlement on the planet. From what I have been told there are currently 2,300 people living on the planet below."

The viewscreen suddenly switched to show a large space station under construction in orbit. It was obvious the StarStrike was moving to match orbits with the station.

"Why is that here?" Jason asked. It was clear that a lot of time and effort had been expended to build the station. "This system is a long ways from Earth. What if the Hocklyns stumble across it?" Looking at the screen, he could see that the finished section of the space station looked to be heavily armed. There were numerous weapons turrets and what he guessed were some type of missile platforms.

"That's why it's here," Admiral Streth replied in a determined voice. "This system is between Earth and the Hocklyns and far enough away so that the Hocklyns should discover it before reaching Earth. We keep the StarStrike and four light cruisers in this system at all times. We have a squadron of long-range stealth shuttles that we use to monitor the systems farther core-ward for any signs of the enemy. Hopefully we will have an advance warning before they arrive here."

"You're not sure about the 268 years, are you?" Jason said, realizing why this system was here. "You built this base to hold up the Hocklyns if they come too soon."

Admiral Streth let out a deep breath. "You're very observant, Commander. We feel pretty comfortable about the 268-year figure, but one of their supposed trading scouts could arrive sooner. If they do, we will make it disappear. We won't make the same mistakes we made last time."

"What exactly are your plans for this system?" Greg asked. He was intrigued by the planet below. What would it feel like to set foot on another world besides Earth?

"We're going to fortify it to the maximum," Admiral Streth replied, determinedly. "It will also serve as a training center for the fleet that I hope we can build with Earth's help. There will be a very powerful defensive grid placed around the planet consisting of railgun and missile platforms. There have also been some suggestions about mine fields, but we don't know how effective they might be against Hocklyn ships. We are going to make this system into a death trap for the Hocklyns."

The viewscreen returned to a view of the peaceful planet below them. Jason could see oceans and even clouds. In many ways, it resembled Earth. He thought about Admiral Streth's words. Here was a man that had led the fight against the Hocklyns for the Human Federation of Worlds. A Federation that no longer existed. Jason hoped that same fate wasn't in Earth's future.

Early the next morning, a large shuttle landed on the edge of the small spaceport next to the human settlement on New Tellus. Jason and Greg stepped out onto a new world never before touched by humans from Earth.

Greg took a deep breath of the fresh air. In the distance, he could hear what sounded like birds calling. He could see a few flying in the air, but they were unlike any birds he had ever seen before. A gentle breeze blew. He could see numerous trees in the distance. Some looked just like trees back on Earth and others were very different. This was like a dream come true. He had actually made it to another world. At that moment, Greg felt as if he was on top of the world. Never in his life had he expected to experience something like this. He looked over at Jason and smiled. He was glad he had made the trip to Ceres.

Admiral Streth looked over at the two Earth humans, guessing what they were experiencing. He would let them enjoy this day. There was so much to show them on this beautiful world. In many ways, it was like Tellus. In the back of his mind, he would always remember the day that his own people had been discovered by the Hocklyns and later how their worlds had met their end. He would do everything in his power to make sure Earth didn't suffer the same fate.

Jason looked around, breathing in the fresh air. The admiral and he had spoken quite a bit on the trip to New Tellus about the current situation on Earth. Both had agreed that the governments of Earth should reveal that an advanced spacecraft had been discovered on the Moon. They would say there were no survivors and that it had crashed there a long time ago. That would allow the technology from the ship to be spread slowly across the planet. There would be no mention of the Hocklyns or the survivors from the Human Federation of Worlds.

Once the people of Earth began to get used to the idea that there could be other races out in the universe, they would begin constructing Earth's first true spaceships. They would be smaller than the Federations and would serve as training platforms. For a few decades, they would be allowed to explore the neighboring stars. Admiral Streth had mentioned to him that there were ten systems with habitable planets within twenty light years of Earth. These ten systems could be colonized and eventually prepared for the coming conflict with the Hocklyns. Given enough time and resources, the Hocklyns when they arrived would face a well armed and determined human race.

Jason hoped they had the time and fortitude to do what was necessary. The Federation people would help, but for the time being it would be behind the scenes and secretive. No one outside of a few carefully chosen people would know about the Federation base inside of Ceres or here on New Tellus.

Jason knew he had his work cut out for him over the next few years. The diplomacy would be left to the politicians, but the Avenger was another matter. Once the surviving section had been repaired, Admiral Streth had suggested expanding the Avenger base. It would make an ideal training center for Earth's future space force. Admiral

Streth had made it clear that he wanted Jason in charge of that base. He also had mentioned that Ariel would demand it anyway.

Looking over at Greg, Jason could see the excited look on his friend's face. They had made it to another world! Someday Greg's son might also be standing here on New Tellus if he joined the future space forces. Jason had a strong suspicion that he would. But for now, all of that was in the future. They were the first Earth humans to set foot on a new world, and he wanted to take advantage of that. For the next few hours, he didn't want to worry about the future.

Admiral Streth felt pretty sure he knew what Jason and Greg were thinking, and he had no intention of spoiling this moment. He watched as the two walked over and stood on the grass next to the landing field. He walked down the ramp and out to where they were standing. "I have arranged for an atmospheric transport to take us around," Admiral Streth informed Jason and Greg. "This is only the second time I have been on this world." Then, with a smile on his face, he added, "Let's explore it together."

The End

Due to numerous requests from fans, I have written a full-length Moon Wreck novel to conclude this part of the Slaver Wars Series. Moon Wreck: Fleet Academy takes place 24 years after the events in Moon Wreck: Secrets of Ceres. It will soon be out in paperback.

If you would like to see this story continue in the Slaver Wars, put up a review with some stars. Good reviews encourage an author to write and help books to sell. Reviews can be just a few short sentences describing what you liked about the book. If you have suggestions, please contact me at my website listed on the following page. Thank you for reading Moon Wreck and being so supportive.

Books in the Slaver War series should be read in the following order.

Moon Wreck
The Slaver Wars: Alien Contact
Moon Wreck: Fleet Academy.
The Slaver Wars: First Strike (October 2013)

The Slaver Wars: Alien Contact can be read either before or after Moon Wreck.

Turn the page to see other books by Raymond L. Weil.

For updates on current writing projects and future publications go to my author website. Sign up for future notifications when new books come out on Amazon.

Website: http://raymondlweil.com/

Other Books by Raymond L. Weil
Available at Amazon

-

Dragon Dreams: Dragon Wars
Dragon Dreams: Gilmreth the Awakening
Dragon Dreams: Snowden the White Dragon
Dragon Dreams: Firestorm Mount (2014)

-

Star One: Tycho City: Discovery
Star One: Neutron Star
Star One: Dark Star
Star One: Tycho City: Survival (December 2013)

-

Moon Wreck
Moon Wreck: Fleet Academy

-

The story continues in

-

The Slaver Wars: Alien Contact
The Slaver Wars: First Strike (October 2013)

-

Turn the page for a quick description of The Slaver Wars: Alien Contact and Moon Wreck: Fleet Academy.

The Slaver Wars: Alien Contact

The 1,200-meter battle cruiser StarStrike slid quietly through empty space. The ship was a Conqueror Class Command Cruiser, one of the most powerful warships ever built by the Human Federation of Worlds. There were only four of the powerful ships of war in the Federation's entire fleet. The StarStrike and its small fleet were on a fact finding mission deep within suspected enemy territory. The 1,500-meter Galaxy Class Battle Carrier Victory was above the StarStrike, along with its four light cruiser escorts. Several small fighter craft flew around the small fleet keeping a constant vigilance for any incoming threats. Two space destroyers were ahead of the fleet scanning for any potential enemy targets. It was essential that the human fleet remain undetected until it had completed its reconnaissance mission.

Fleet Admiral Hedon Streth sat at his command console watching the main viewscreen on the front wall of the Command Center. He was of medium build, and his dark hair was just starting to turn gray on the sides. The admiral was forty-two years old, and the worry lines on his face showed that he had been through a lot the past few months. Months he would like to forget. It had been a trying and desperate time for the entire human race.

The viewscreen showed unwinking stars ahead, and the scanners and long-range sensors were free of threats. The Command Center was in the shape of a rectangle, and its twenty-crew personnel were efficiently going about their jobs. At the reinforced security hatch, two heavily armed marines stood guard. No one entered the Command Center without the proper clearance. Two more similarly armed marines stood just outside the hatch in the corridor. Security now was much more obvious than a few short months ago.

"Still nothing," Colonel Amanda Sheen, the executive officer, spoke. She was standing next to the holographic plotting table, which showed the present fleet disposition and the CAP fighters that were flying their routine patrol routes. She was currently checking the large tactical screens above her as well as the information appearing on the table.

"Confirm mission status," ordered Admiral Streth, letting out a deep breath and shifting his gaze from the viewscreen to his executive officer.

They had picked this system hoping it would be clear of enemy activity. Their mission was extremely sensitive, and the security of the Human Federation of Worlds depended upon its success. Hedon felt the full weight of that responsibility on his shoulders and knew that this mission just had to succeed. Failure was not an option. The entire Federation was in extreme danger, and this mission might well determine the future of humankind in the galaxy.

"Navigation, I want a position status report," Colonel Sheen barked, her blue eyes turning toward the two officers sitting at the main navigation console.

"We are currently one hundred and eighteen astronomical units out from the target system's primary. Fleet is currently moving in system at eighteen percent speed of light on sublight engines," replied the chief navigation officer.

"What do we have on the long-range sensors?" Sheen asked over her mini-com, glancing over at the large scanning and sensor console, which was manned by two fleet officers. She wore a small communications device in her right ear, which allowed her to contact any station on the ship in an instant.

"System has two planets," Lieutenant Stalls reported smoothly as he checked the latest information coming in on his computer screens. "Both are gas giants in distant orbits. No asteroid fields or moons detected. System is absent of any artificial emissions."

"System is as we had hoped," reported Colonel Sheen turning to face the admiral. "There are no signs of any enemy vessels, and the system has no significant resources to attract any type of mining or scientific activity."

Admiral Streth nodded his head in acknowledgement. He knew that Amanda was a highly qualified officer graduating in the top ten percent of her class at the fleet academy. She was a brunette with a trim figure and thirty-two years of age. She was also a firm disciplinarian. The crew respected her, and she was everything he could ask for in an executive officer.

"Get me the Victory, I think it's time we get some information about this area of space," ordered Admiral Streth, reaching a decision. They had been moving steadily deeper into suspected Hocklyn space for the last eight weeks. "It's time we launch the stealth scouts and find out what's out there."

Colonel Sheen nodded. This was their mission and she was ready to get it started. Glancing back at the sensor and scanner screens, she noted that they were clearly empty of any hostile threats. That needed to continue for several more days if they hoped for any chance of success. Looking around the Command Center, she could sense the heightened vibrancy in the crew at the admiral's announcement to begin the actual mission.

On board the Victory, Commander Adler listened as the admiral ordered the launch of the stealth scouts. The Victory had six of the highly advanced scout ships on board, which were nearly undetectable to normal methods of scanning. It was hoped that the Hocklyns would have no way to detect the small surveillance vessels. Their entire mission and the safety of their fleet depended on it.

Adler ended the communication with the admiral and turned to his executive officer Major Timmins. "I want all six scout ships ready to launch ASAP. Mission is a go."

"Finally," responded Major Timmins letting out a deep breath and then announcing over his mini-com, "All stations stand by for scout ship launch. Mission is a go. Flight bay, begin launch preparations."

Instantly the tension and excitement in the Command Center notched up. This was what everyone had been waiting for. It was time to find out just how large the Hocklyn Empire was and how big a threat they were to the Federation.

Commander Adler turned toward the lieutenant in charge of Navigation. "I want a list of the twenty nearest stars that are capable of supporting life-bearing planets."

"Yes, sir," the young blonde replied as she began entering commands into her computer.

Lieutenant Ashton was rated as one of the top navigators in the entire fleet. She also held an advanced degree in Stellar Cartography. She had written an impressive thesis on deep space navigation her senior year at the fleet academy on Tellus.

Down below in the main flight bay, the six scout ships were brought up on elevators from their secure hangars beneath. The ships were covered in a layer of dark composite material that the scientists swore would be impervious to Hocklyn scans. Power sources were muffled, and the ships were built to present a minimal profile to enemy ships.

Each scout could carry a six-man crew and were capable of operating independently of the fleet for eight to ten days. They had FTL drives as well as powerful sublight engines. The ships were wedge shaped with gentle curves. Each was twenty-two meters long and twelve meters wide. Weapons consisted of six Hunter anti-fighter missiles hidden inside the wings and two medium lasers in the nose. The nose lasers were a recent development and had been added at the last minute to the scouts. The pilots were still arguing whether the lasers were an improvement over the 30 mm cannons they had replaced.

Technicians quickly checked over all six ships, making sure they were ready for their missions. The ships had been kept on standby for nearly two weeks. A quick check and all the scouts were deemed ready for immediate launch. The deck chief notified flight control that all six scouts were mission ready.

Flight control was at the far end of the massive flight bay. Large reinforced glass windows looked out over the bay allowing the controllers inside to see the activity in the bay. Inside flight control was a hum of busy activity as men and women watched their consoles and kept track of all the activity going on inside the bay as well as outside. The CAG was standing next to the flight operations officer at the main control console. Across the back wall, numerous viewscreens depicted activity inside the bay. Several large scanner screens showed the flight space around the fleet and the current locations of the CAP fighters that were out on patrol.

Activating his mini-com, the CAG gave the order for the flight crews to board their scouts. The technicians were finished, now it would be up to the highly trained crews to begin their mission and bring home the information the Federation so desperately needed.

The waiting crews quickly made their way into their respective vessels. They had been in the pilot's ready room, hoping this star system would be secure enough so they could start their covert mission. Nerves had been getting on edge and tempers had been flaring as they moved farther away from the Federation and deeper into what was suspected to be Hocklyn controlled space. They all felt relieved and energized that it was finally time to launch the mission.

Captain Karl Arcles settled down into his pilot's seat in one of the scouts and looked over at his copilot, Lieutenant Lacy Sanders. The young twenty-six-year-old blonde looked slightly pale. It was one thing to train for this type of mission; it was another to actually do it.

"Nothing to be nervous about Lieutenant," Arcles said with a reassuring smile. "Just treat this as a routine flight. We've done this often enough in practice."

"Yes, sir," replied Lieutenant Sanders taking a deep breath. Lacy could feel her heart racing. She looked over at Captain Arcles and said nervously. "Only this time it's for real, and what we find may determine the future of the entire human race. I know they said the Hocklyns shouldn't be able to detect our scout ships. We all know that the Hocklyn's technology level is higher than ours. What if the experts are wrong?"

Arcles leaned back in his seat and didn't reply. The lieutenant was correct. The future of humanity's home system and its four outlying colony worlds rested on what this mission discovered about the Hocklyns. The Hocklyns had attacked the Human Federation of Worlds without provocation. Millions of innocent people had died in the brutal attack.

The mission of this fleet was to find out just how large an empire the Hocklyns controlled, and what could be done to prevent future attacks. Was it just a few worlds as the Federation government hoped, or was it a large galaxy-spanning empire? The Hocklyns held a decisive edge in technology. That had already been determined from the technologies on their ships. Did they also hold a decisive edge in population as well as natural resources? Karl just hoped the experts were right and the scout ships were undetectable.

"Launch at your discretion, Captain Arcles." The CAG's voice came over the com system. "Good luck and good hunting."

"Let's get the systems powered up," ordered Arcles glancing over at Lieutenant Sanders. "It's time to get this show on the road."

It only took the two a few minutes to finish powering up the small ship and complete their final preflight checks. The techs had already checked everything earlier, so it was mainly a matter of flipping a few switches and powering up the sublight drive.

"Everything shows green," Lieutenant Sanders reported as she tightened her safety harness. She closed her eyes briefly and said a short prayer. This mission frightened her. They were so far away from home, and if anything happened, they would be on their own. No one would be coming to save them.

Captain Arcles reached forward, taking the scout ship's controls. A moment later, the little ship darted out from the flight bay and moved away from the majestic battle carrier. "Insert first FTL coordinates," he ordered, looking over at Sanders. He had flown with the lieutenant often enough that he knew that once the mission began she would calm down. She was a very capable officer; she just needed to learn to control her anxiety.

The lieutenant tapped a few commands into her navigation computer and then nodded as she double-checked the results. "Coordinates locked in."

Arcles nodded and turned the controls over to the ship's flight computer. He watched as the FTL timer began counting down and soon neared zero. The other scout ships didn't show on the small ship's scanners and sensors, but he knew they were out there.

"Standby for FTL insertion," Arcles spoke over the com to the other crewmembers. There were two mission specialists in the cockpit behind him who were responsible for the scout's sensors and stealth systems. Two more technicians were back in the small crew compartment.

Moments later, a spatial vortex of blue-white light appeared directly in front of the curved nose of the scout ship. The scout ship darted into the vortex, which instantly vanished, leaving no sign of the scout. Within a few minutes, the other five scouts had vanished in the same way. Each scout had a different set of destinations to search.

Admiral Streth watched as the six scout ships vanished into the blue-white vortexes of light. He let out a deep breath and wondered about what they would find. They were nearly six hundred light years from home, and in what was believed to be enemy territory. The entire outcome of the war might very well rest on what the scouts discovered.

"It's begun," Colonel Sheen commented quietly, seeing that the six blips representing the scouts had vanished from her plotting table. They had been tracked by high-resolution cameras as they left the Victory.

In a way, she felt relieved that the mission had finally been launched. Not knowing what the Federation actually faced had been gnawing fearfully in the pit of her stomach for quite some time. Amanda just wanted her parents to be safe back home on Aquaria. Recent events had made her extremely concerned for her parents' safety.

Colonel Sheen pursed her lips, feeling apprehensive at what the scouts might discover. When she had entered the fleet academy, she had never dreamed she would become part of an interstellar war. That

146

was something that only happened on the holo vids or in books. Her parents lived on the colony of Beltran Three, called Aquaria by its inhabitants. The planet was nearly eighty percent water and possessed the most beautiful ocean beaches of any of the four major colonies. Amanda knew that the orbital defenses above her home planet were being heavily strengthened to protect the colony from another Hocklyn attack. She just prayed that it would be enough and that her parents would remain safe.

"Mission counter has started," she reported as a timer began moving on the plotting table. "First system emergence should occur in twenty-two minutes."

Admiral Streth nodded. "I want the fleet kept at Condition Two. We don't know how well the stealth protection on those scouts will hold up. If the Hocklyns detect them, we could have their warships here soon after."

"Yes, sir," responded Colonel Sheen, hoping that was not the case. She walked several paces over to a set of consoles manned by two lieutenants and two ensigns. "Keep all weapon systems on standby. If any unknowns are detected, I want firing solutions yesterday!"

Lieutenant Jacobs instantly responded. "All targets will be locked upon FTL emergence until deemed friendly or unfriendly."

Colonel Sheen nodded and passed the same order over her mini-com to the rest of the fleet after setting her com to fleet-wide so she could communicate the admiral's orders to the other ship commanders. She then continued to walk from console to console in the Command Center, talking to the men and women who manned them. At the helm control console, she ordered Lieutenant Jenikens to be prepared for emergency maneuvers upon her command if they went to Condition One.

Satisfied that everything was as ready as it could be, she returned to her station at the plotting table. She could have done the same thing over her mini-com, which connected her to all the stations, but she preferred to talk to the individual crewmembers whenever possible. She felt it made a better impression upon them.

Admiral Streth had watched Colonel Sheen move through the Command Center talking to the crew. He leaned back in his seat, thinking about what had brought them to this point. It had all started eight months back when a strange vessel had entered the Stalor System, which contained a small mining operation. The miners had instantly screamed for help when their scanners had detected an alien ship going into orbit above the volcanic moon they were mining. It was the first alien ship ever encountered by the Federation.

-

Read the rest of this story in (The Slaver Wars: Alien Contact).

http://www.amazon.com/dp/B00CEQ9KB8/ref=cm_sw_su_dp

Turn the page for a brief description of Moon Wreck: Fleet Academy.

Moon Wreck: Fleet Academy

The starship New Horizon is Earth's first attempt at an FTL capable spaceship, but others don't want the mission to succeed. The mission goes suddenly and horribly wrong with the possibility of inadvertently leading the Hocklyns to Earth, decades in advance of their estimated arrival time. Can the cadets on the New Horizon stop the deadly plot before it's too late?

The Federation survivors on Ceres have constructed a new warship. It's the most powerful ship they have ever built. Its mission is simple, return to the old Federation worlds, search for survivors, and find out how far the Hocklyn Slave Empire has spread. The whole key to their mission is secrecy, but the disastrous events on the New Horizon may jeopardize everything.

http://www.amazon.com/dp/B00DUQ1BY0

ABOUT THE AUTHOR

I live in Clinton Oklahoma with my wife of 38 years and our cats. I attended college at SWOSU in Weatherford Oklahoma, majoring in Math with minors in Creative Writing and History.

My hobbies include watching soccer, reading, camping, and of course writing. I coached youth soccer for twelve years before moving on and becoming a high school soccer coach for thirteen more. I also enjoy playing with my three grandchildren. I also have a very vivid imagination, which sometimes worries my friends. They never know what I am going to say or what I am going to do.

I am an avid reader and have a science fiction / fantasy collection of over two thousand paperbacks. I want future generations to know the experience of reading a good book as I have over the last forty years.

Made in the USA
Lexington, KY
18 March 2015